TRIASSIC

By

PHIL BARTOW

ISBN: 0983517606
ISBN-13: 9780983517603

Climber and explorer Roy Graham is drawn into a globe-hopping search for possible sources of man's beginning.

Characters and places are mainly fictitious. Some events, like an 1800-foot wave in Lituya Bay, Alaska are real. Some of the concepts might come about in the future.

All misrepresentations of good science are mine.

Phil Bartow
1999

TRIASSIC

(CONTENTS)

-PROLOG-

Science is storytelling with a purpose. Science stories have predictive value and guide exploration on land and in laboratories. Over time some stories are elaborated and others discredited. The genius of man is the ability to spin stories on limited observations and to create new stories when there are gaps in understanding and when expected endings are discredited.

CHAPTER 1
NETS

The morning sun was touching the peaks and casting shadows into the fog filled steep jungle canyons in the southern Andes. A helicopter was slowly moving up into the higher elevations. It stayed low following the valley floors until the valley ended below a towering peak. It then rose over the flanking side of the valley and dropped into the next valley. Rodrigues Valtrone, the pilot, followed the terrain to nearly 18,000 feet before breaking out over a flat, rock-strewn, barren plateau that stretched for miles to the North. The western boundary of the plateau was lined with snow covered peaks rising over 21,000 feet.

The helicopter landed briefly. There was no hint that the plateau was sliced by hundreds of narrow, deep canyons with jungle covered walls. Fifty feet above the plateau surface, the terrain looked like it had sharp wrinkles.

From a higher elevation the view of the plateau was that of a green labyrinthine maze two thousand feet deep.

Rodrigues took the helicopter to altitude fifteen feet above the plateau and skimmed along the surface going north. At this altitude they avoided any radar that might exist.

As the helicopter flew along the flat surface of the plateau it would pass over a fog-filled void and drop twenty to thirty feet because of the loss of the air under the blades pushing against the ground. Rodrigues had to increase the engine speed to compensate for the loss of ground effect and force the helicopter up before he reached the wall on the opposite side of the void seconds later. "If we go down in here," he said to himself out loud, "there is no way of finding our way out. There are no maps of the area and no communications in the deep canyon."

He flew two miles and passed over three canyons. "We are at the coordinates," he said.

"We see you on the screen, Roddy. Looks good. Start down."

"Roger that, Iceburg," Rodrigues answered and started a slow descent. At this altitude maneuverability was difficult. Two guns were mounted on the left side. The gun operators methodically scanned the near-vertical cliffs.

The voice crackled in the pilot's earphones. "We've lost two groups in there in the last three weeks. The second was a rescue effort. That is two helicopters and ten men."

The pilot is talking to a geologist at their home base on the Antarctic.

Mark Stark, Chief Geologist for Global Oil Exploration, sat in front of two computer screens. "Roddy," he said into the headset he was wearing, "The static is building. If you lose me pop back up for a few seconds so we can coordinate." Mark raises his eyes from the computer screens and looks up at the gray corrugated steel liner of his Quonset hut buried under the ice.

Bob Grant, the operations manager for the Antarctic base camp for GOE, sat across the room looking through a microscope at thin slices of rock. "Tell them to stay below Chilean radar. We don't have permission to be there."

"Relax Bob, they know that."

"Roddy, where did you go? We lost your GPS coordinates."

Rodrigues took the helicopter up to the ridgeline just below the level of the plateau. "The walls here are so steep and the orientation is such that once we drop two hundred feet below the ridge line we lose the Global Positioning Satellite connection. Those satellites don't look straight down. We might as well be under water. Just remember our last position after you lose our position. I'll pop up when we jump into the next canyon."

A mist rose from the trees carpeting the slopes. The morning sun cast a chopper shadow onto the mist like a projector. Something flashed in the next valley. Craig Ehrin, the machine gun operator shouted, "Did you see that, something reflecting, shiny, over there?"

The pilot rises over the ridge and drops down. "Where?"

"A little lower."

"I don't see anything except some patches of wet rock," Rodrigues says. "Looks like slabs of mica. Only sun reflecting off a wet cliff."

"Whoa," Craig shouts. "There is another flash down there on the shadow side. See it?"

Bart Woldonski scans the area.

"What do you find?" Craig says, "There has to be something there."

The chopper descended further below the ridgeline and moved sideways lower to the other side of the chasm. Bart patiently scanned the futuristic looking device mounted on a gun turret back and forth. "We don't scan a thing."

"Do you have the right patterns?" Mark asked from the ice-bound Quonset hut.

"We calibrated before we left this morning," Bart answered, "Ten patterns."

"Switch over to IR."

Bart turned a knob and set the lock switch above the decal that read DNAS/INFRARED to ON and continued the scan.

"Some small signatures moving around pretty fast, down there, one-hundred-fifty feet. They have to be monkeys. It's vertical and covered with trees and vines. What else could move that fast?"

Mark Stark had been listening to the conversation in the helicopter and turned the headset switch to play through speakers in the room so Bob could hear. "Get in as close as you can," Mark said to Rodrigues.

"If I get any closer the blades will turn green."

The radio starts to break up. The canyon walls are interfering with transmission.

The chopper descended deeper in the green void.

Bart shouts, "There is nothing down here. Even the monkeys have disappeared from the IR screen."

"What caused the flash?" Rodrigues asked.

Craig shrugged his shoulders. "Maybe it was reflection off the window projecting onto a shiny leaf or something. Maybe I imagined it."

"If we go any deeper we won't have much room to maneuver except vertical," Rodrigues says.

The static in Rodrigues' headset started to dominate.

"Go up the valley a ways," Mark says. "Then try the next valley. I think that is where Wayne's chopper went down."

Rodrigues said, "Mark, I can barely hear what you are saying through the static. Say again, you are breaking…" Before he can finish the sentence with "up" he looked to his left and was startled by what he saw. "What the hell," he murmured. Then he shouted, "NETS!"

Huge nets shot out from the jungle cliffs, like those thrown by fishermen. They flew out from both sides of the narrow chasm and descend on the helicopter's blades. The blades broke rocks fastened to the edges of the nets. The main rotor tangled in the ropes and rocks. The tail rotor jammed and the helicopter started to spin wildly. It rotated three times before hitting trees on the sunny side of the canyon walls. Helicopter number three started a steep crash into the narrow valley floor two thousand feet below.

At the listening station the crackling static stopped.

Mark looked at Bob, "With his accent and the static– did he say 'nuts' or 'nets?'"

CHAPTER 2
REORGANIZATION

"Welcome back, Juan. How was your vacation?" Roy Graham looked up from the maps on his desk as Juan Martinez entered the office of Outdoor Adventures. "Three weeks in the Caribbean must have been nice."

"Yeah, right, three weeks would have been nice! Too bad it turned into three years. Anyway, boss, you said I should come by when I got back and here I am, just a little late."

Three years ago Juan had returned to his parent's home in Jamaica to recuperate from a disastrous glacier expedition with Outdoor Adventures. A few days before his scheduled return, he married the girl next door, whose monthly period hadn't returned on schedule either. Just for consistency, he supposed, no baby ever appeared. Juan had the kind of dogged loyalty that kept him trying to be a decent husband, but he fairly soon remembered why his wife had been the girl he'd left behind in the first place.

When a more recent and wealthier arrival from the states appeared, Juan was not very jealous and very relieved to hear she wanted a divorce.

"What are the maps for?" Juan looked over Roy's shoulder.

"I've got a couple of trips to plan. Want to go?"

"If there are glaciers the answer is no!" Juan sounded emphatic. "I'd forgotten how much I don't like snow anymore. The one good thing about the last three years was the sun."

"Juan, that glacier trip was three years ago. We have to get you back on snow."

"You would have better luck getting me back on Matilda."

"So how is you former wife?"

"Don't know, don't care. Who with?"

"Who with?" Roy repeated Juan's last question.

"Trips! The ones your maps are for!"

"Oh these," Roy pointed to the maps in front of him. "I've been out to Wallace Images."

"My ears must still be plugged from the plane flight," Juan erupted, "I can't believe I heard that. A trip with Wallace would be a double no for me. Our last one with them had glaciers plus five murders. I can't believe you'd go anywhere near them. You barely got out alive last time."

The clients for Outdoor Adventures varied from drug abuse rehabilitation programs to management teams in large corporations. Three years ago the president of Wallace Images had hired Roy to take the senior staff on an outing in which they had to work together as a team. It was a two-week trip across Alaskan glaciers that ended in catastrophe when one of Roy's guides was exposed as an industrial spy. His reaction launched an escalating spiral of suspicions, betrayals and revenge that led to five deaths. One of the victims was Raymond Wallace, founder of Wallace Imaging.

"Wallace Images," Roy responded defensively, "has reorganized and consolidated their staff. James, Raymond's brother, is president now. They've converted the production building to office space and leased the building to other companies. They all use Wallace computers and imaging technology, especially WIGS, the Wallace Imaging Global Simulator. I met people from some of those companies. None of them was as gung-ho for outdoor challenges as Raymond Wallace, but they did want some kind of outing."

Juan shook his head. "I don't do snow."

"Relax Juan," Roy said,"I thought a couple of week end rock climbing trips would be good starters. No snow, yet."

"Okay, Okay count me in. I need to start earning some money, might as well be outdoors! So just out of morbid curiosity, what is happening at Wallace Images? And what is WIGS?"

The phone rang. "Juan," out of old habit Juan answered the office phone, "Roy? Sure hang on. It's for you boss. Some guy named Mark."

"Stark?"

"That's him."

"Mark," Roy, said catching the phone Juan tossed him. "Where are you? McGurdo Bay?" Roy listened and answered. "Can I go climbing day after tomorrow? Sure, can you? You are eight thousand miles away. Go for it. Where do we meet? Did you say Hanger 24 at McCord? Okay, call when you are an hour out. Is that okay? See you when you get here." Roy tossed the cordless phone back to Juan.

"He is eight thousand miles away and is going to go climbing with you day after tomorrow."

"He says he has a real fast plane. I wonder what he wants. What ever it is, "It's" urgent."

"Ok, guess you'll find out tomorrow. Meanwhile, what is WIGS?" As usual Juan pursued his own one-track train of thought.

"A new type of display. It stands for "Wallace Imaging Global Simulator." It looks like a six-foot balloon with the oceans and continents painted on it. It is really an expandable hologram. I was only given a short review. But I can tell you it is impressive."

"It must be, to impress you. I'm beginning to see what's pulling you back to Wallace Imaging. Meanwhile, now that we're talking about possible income producing activity, what do these new tenants do, the ones that want to take trips?"

"TECTSIM is a group that is simulating the formation of the earth. They are building models of tectonic plate movement and mountain building. One of their objectives is to understand earthquake processes. They are also interested in vulcanology. They gather a lot of data from lasers scattered all around the globe to detect slight crustal movement. They want to use WIGS as their data storage and modeling facility.

"The people at TECTSIM are basically geologists. They all have had field experience. We can probably do more advanced climbing with them. We might even ask them where they want to go. I think some of them want to check the lasers on the summits of Everest and K2."

"Can't do that. Glaciers."

"Relax Juan. They don't have time for that anyway."

"Who else?"

"GENEG is a company developing data base storage and search procedures for genome mapping. They're interested in historical genome migration."

"Do these genomes bite?"

"No, no, Juan," Roy laughed, "Genome research involves mapping human genes patterns. Heredity and all that stuff."

"Okay. What kind of people?"

"Mostly medical lab types with soft hands, soft butts from lots of hours sitting in front of computers. They also do DNA testing for crime labs. Their work gets pretty sensitive. Wallace Images buildings are surrounded by fences and there is a guard gate. It is secure."

Juan had walked around the four-by-eight plywood platform Roy was using for a worktable. Standing next to Roy he oriented a piece of paper so he could read it. "Who are these guys, RENGCA?"

"They are the "Renegade Cultural Anthropologists," a bunch of guys who are outside the box of contemporary thought. They are developing simulations of cultural migration. They are using stochastic processes to see how known archeological sites fit possible migration patterns. They don't think that man necessarily started in Africa and migrated north and east over the Bering Straits, down through North America and eventually to the tip of South America. Ancient sites in the southern end of South America are older than the oldest in North America."

"What kind of shape are they in?"

Roy realized he was very glad to have Juan back. One thing he'd always liked about Juan was his steady focus on the individuals on their trips. A person's rank or status in life did not affect Juan. He simply saw the person in front of him within the context of the task they were doing. He knew what kinds of challenges they might get into on a climb, or caving. He certainly knew what could happen on a simple glacier walk. Juan was concerned with what physical shape a person was in. He had usually been in charge of fitting people with boots, pants, parkas and packs. Attitudes and bad behavior were like rain and weather. He knew it was there but didn't try to change it. He knew there were reasons that people behaved the way they did. Juan's primary concern was whether their behavior would lead to trouble. When someone started to bully him, he would say "Sitting under a snow cornice is not a good way to stay out of the rain," and then walk away. The antagonist would be left wondering "What the hell does that mean?" as he watched Juan's receding back.

Roy returned to Juan's question about RENGCA: "They are an odd lot. Some are museum types that play with bones. Some are field researchers."

"Like, lie in the sand and scrape fossils with toothpicks?"

"Right. Most of them are internationally known but their work at RENGCA is kept quiet. They are trying to shoot down some generally accepted concepts and are trying to avoid the heat until they have the evidence they need. They have the motto, 'Copernicus died for our Ignorance.'"

Two days later Roy drove up to the west gate at McCord Air Force base thirty-five miles south of Seattle and asked the guard for directions to hanger 24. The guard stiffened slightly and said, "SIR, I will have to see your identification and authorization, SIR!"

Roy sensed that he had tripped a precautionary wire. Normally access onto the base required only photo identification, driver's license, if that, and the salutation was a friendly "Sir." This request was formal and military.

Roy fished his wallet from his left hip pocket and extracted an identification card from a hidden flap. He handed the guard the card. The guard stared at it, turned it over, and then back to the front side. He looked at Roy's face from two angles then snapped to attention, handed Roy the card, and said, Honored, General, SIR. Go straight to runway one, turn right and go to the end of the field, SIR. Pass SIR!" He saluted.

Roy acknowledged the salute and the guard lowered his right arm. Roy accelerated toward the runway.

It was rare that his military identity was exposed. His love of adventure and challenge had moved him into Special Forces training. Over a number of years he had made friends with military leaders he respected. They all were on the leading edge of surveillance technology. Roy's specialty had been secreting new devices into enemy camps and strongholds and he was still called on occasionally to consult. He was also still technically General Roy P. Graham. Because of the nature of his work only a few military people knew him and protected his identity. If Mark had hinted he would be arriving in a secured hanger, Roy would not have asked at the gate where the hanger was located.

This was the first time in three years that any hint of military association had surfaced. The last time was when General Parker had flown in the Coast Guard helicopter that extracted Roy from the log strewn Pacific Ocean. Roy had been fighting an industrial spy on a fishing boat in Lituya Bay in Alaska. A wave generated by an earthquake and landslide carried the forest washed off a mountain slope and Roy's boat into the ocean.

Mark Stark was standing in front of Hangar 24 when Roy drove up. "How did you get a ride in the X-35?" Roy asked Mark. "It's a classified prototype. Impressive."

"If it is so classified, how do you know about it and how did you get into the hanger? Sir!"

"Smartass!"

"My boss pulled some strings. Jet chopper from McGurdo Bay to the Falklands and Mach two and Mach three from there. I bet all the vessels in my eyeballs are bloodshot."

"Are you after a big climb?"

"Not necessarily. I just want to get off the ice for a couple of hours. I'm not sure how much time I have for relaxing. Maybe we can do something simple like hike up Mount Si. A couple of hours up and down."

Mount Si is a peak on the West Side of the Cascade Range in Washington, thirty miles east of Seattle. The west face rises steeply, three thousand feet above North Bend. A four-mile hiking trail switches back and forth across the south and east slopes. On a clear day, from the three-hundred-foot bald rock summit known as the haystack, the tall buildings of Seattle can be seen to the west with the Olympic Mountains beyond.

"Si is fine. It's not a weekend so there won't be a line of people and dogs from one end of the trail to the other." The drive from McCord to North Bend took fifty-five minutes. The two men drove in silence to the peak thirty miles east of Seattle.

As they began the four-mile hiking trail with its back and forth across the slopes, Mark made no mention of his reason for visiting Roy. They reminisced about other climbs and a couple of mutual friends.

"I was watching reruns of a TV series a few months back called 'Twin-Peaks.' A mountain behind the town had a summit that looked like Mt. Si," Mark said puffing a little.

"It was. Weird program. A prelude to the X-Files in a couple of ways. Paranormal events and David Duchovny. A bit of suspense and mystery."

It was a two-hour hike to the base of the rock summit and a fifteen-minute scramble up a rock gully to a small ridge, then twenty feet more to the summit. North Bend stretched beneath them, out around the base for several miles. Two ribbons of concrete stretched from Snoqualmie Pass to the east through the southern side of North Bend and disappeared in the direction of Seattle. The overcast and clouds blocked the view of the skyscrapers. It wasn't raining, but a light mist condensed on their clothing.

The two men enjoyed the scenery for ten minutes without speaking. A cawing raven chased another from the rocky ridges below. A small pika, a gerbil-sized rodent, popped in and out of the cavities in the rocks, tugging on Roy's shoe. The deep popping of compression brakes on a logging truck echoed below them. The hills to the north, east and south were a patchwork of old-growth trees and clear-cut fields dotted with stumps.

"I'm wondering if you can help us?" Mark said slowly. "We've lost three helicopters and fourteen people, good people, in three weeks. It happened in a very steep mountainous area on the southern border of Chile and Argentina, south of Aconcagua. We don't how or where exactly. The first trip was a quick exploration without government permission. It is a very remote area and the chopper stayed below the radar levels. The canyon walls are so steep and narrow that satellite-based GPS tracking capabilities were blocked. We knew generally where they were but the Lojack coordinates were lost when they descended two hundred feet below the ridgeline. There is something about the mineral content of the area and the steepness of the canyons that blocks radio contact when the chopper drops into the canyons. The second chopper went in to try and find the first. We armed a third chopper with machine gun, bio-scanning system and metal detectors. It disappeared the same way the others did."

"Have you contacted the Chilean authorities?"

"No. It's not uncommon for exploration companies to make impromptu and unauthorized flights to check out a geologic site. It is getting trickier these days because of drug traffic by air. If the government finds out we will be hung out to dry for weeks and might have problems getting exploration permits if we do find something."

"Is there a chance you were brought down by armed drug camps?"

"Anything is possible. We think the area is too remote for an effective drug operation. We didn't find life signs except for some monkeys and even those were sporadic."

"Roy, what are the chances we could go in by foot? You've climbed all kinds of peaks and foraged in the jungle. Could you lead a team to the bottom of the canyon where we know the choppers went down and try to find out what happened to them?"

"You flew eight thousand miles to ask me to go on an adventure in the death zone?" Roy mimicked the Twilight Zone theme song "Nee-noo-nee-noo".

"Not just that. Next week is your birthday and I wanted to bring you a present. Here." Mark reached into his pack and pulled out a little wooden box and handed it to Roy.

Roy opened the two-inch by six-inch polished mahogany box. Inside was a cylinder of white rock with large areas of brown and black and hints of pink. "Core sample from the Antarctic?"

"Yep, with a twist."

"Which is?"

"We drilled that site because of the DNA content of the rock."

"DNA? Like in double helix, O.J. Simpson and genome mapping?"

"Yes."

"Sounds interesting. Tell me more about this when we get off this rock. In the morning I want you to show me the last known positions of the choppers that went down."

Mark reached into his pack and pulled out a map.

Roy said, "Not here. Besides I want to use some high-tech equipment of my own to locate where your crews went down. It will be dark when we get down. You need sleep. In the morning we'll go out to Wallace Images and I'll show you the map equivalent of that X-35!"

CHAPTER 3
WIGS

Roy and Mark drove north of downtown Seattle toward the site of a former military base, Ft Lawton. In the early sixties a number of decommissioned military bases were sold or made available for community projects. The Ft Lawton site sat high on a sandy clay bluff, overlooked Puget Sound and to the west, Bainbridge Island and the Olympic Mountains. The site became the location for DayBreak Star, a Native American cultural center, and several high technology companies. The Wallace Research Center started as one building on the northern edge of Ft. Lawton and acquired additional space with the decommissioning. Two buildings were added to what became the Wallace Research Center. The original building became the administration building and the location of their primary product WIGS, Wallace Images Global Simulator. The second building was the research center where the WIGS prototype was developed. WIGS was an outgrowth of the three-dimensional holographic imaging technology that Wallace had developed. The original focus of Wallace Images research was underwater communication and guidance systems. As business expanded, the research activity was moved to a new building. The president, Raymond Wallace, kept what he called "a Wallace technology museum" in the first building, which contained operational displays of products they had developed. The third building was added to the complex when Wallace Images was awarded a substantial contract to manufacture communication devices. Manufacturing problems and losses in competitive bidding for other contracts led Raymond Wallace to hire Roy for a team building outdoor challenge outing in Alaska. Raymond Wallace and Tom Gilmore, the head of research, and several others were killed on the trip. Afterwards the company was restructured. The focus was on research and to support research by other companies that could use WIGS. All of Wallace Imaging activity returned to the first building and the other two were leased to other companies.

Roy drove past a totem pole at the entrance to DayBreak Star and through a wooded area that opened to a large park-like clearing. Both sides of the quarter mile of road that led to a guard shack and enclosing fence were lined with people and posters.

"SAVE THE WHALES," "WHALES BELONG TO THE EARTH, NOT THE MILITARY..."

"What is this all about?" Mark asked.

"NOAA has a project that displays whale migration on WIGS. The whales are tracked from data logging devices that transmit data whenever the whale surfaces. The transmission goes to a satellite and into WIGS. A reporter for the TIMES suggested the data was used for military purposes and crowds started forming."

"Here we are." Roy stopped at the small brick building with thick glass windows. A sign read "Private Property No Trespassing." There was no name or address. The two cameras at either end of the building silently adjusted and triangulated on Roy's face. A guard stepped out of the building. Roy lowered his window and extended his hand. "Hi, Clem. Mark here is a friend and secure."

"Good to see you, Mr. Graham." He shook hands with Roy and looked at Mark, "Mr. Stark. Mr. Wallace said you were coming. Have a good day."

Roy pulled away from the gate.

"I thought you said Mr. Wallace was killed in Alaska."

"James Wallace is Raymond's younger brother. He was Vice-President at the time of the trip." Roy drove past two glass faced buildings reflecting early morning, low puffy clouds, pink high cirrus and blue sky. He parked in front of a four-story dull obsidian cube. The building had no windows and didn't seem to reflect light. A single small red triangle marked the boundary of a possible entrance. There was no walk to the triangle. "Just walk toward the triangle, toward the triangle," Roy said. "There is a walk but a display of grass covers it."

Mark took a step toward the door from the edge of the parking lot and several feet of concrete appeared on the ground in front of him.

"Water, Enter," Roy said and an image of the surface of a lake appeared in front of Mark.

Mark stopped and looked down at fish swimming under his feet.

"Keep walking," Roy said. "Get used to the fact you can walk on water."

"What is this?"

"You are standing on one of the original Wallace Image products, a hologram panel. You will see more of them inside."

Mark walked forward tentatively. Three steps from where he thought the door was going to be, an archway opened and he looked into a bright lobby. The walls were covered with large panels with views of scenic and historic sites from around the world. Above the scenes the windows and the four-story-high skylight ceiling opened to the pink cirrus clouds and blue sky.

"These are too vivid to be paintings and I know we are not there." Mark observed. "Are these more holographic panels?"

"Everything is. This room is only two stories high and has green walls. All the walls and ceiling can be programmed." Roy walked past the security desk and placed his hand on a dull frost-colored pane. A door that had a model of the earth above it appeared to his left.

Roy and Mark walked through the opened door into a hallway that extended ten feet to either side. Roy took a right, walked the ten feet and made a left into a long circular corridor. The inside of the corridor appeared to be divided into a number of rooms. There were doors every thirty feet and next to each door a place for a window that was filled in with the fabric pattern that covered the walls. A panel in front of them was labeled "Schedule." A slot on the panel said "10:30 Hurricane Socrates." The digital clock above the panel displayed 10:15.

"Good," Roy said. "We can catch a few minutes of a simulation of the hurricane that is off the Florida coast. We have some time scheduled after that."

"Will we be listed on the schedule board?" Mark asked.

"No. The board will be blank. If it is blank only the teams running WIGS will be able to observe. There is a lot of military classified and industrially sensitive data processed here."

"Tight security?"

"Very. Every heartbeat of every person in the building is monitored. Remember that cool breeze you felt when we entered the building?"

"Right."

"You were tagged with an aerosol tracker. Sensors in the building track your movements. To get a urine analysis, take a pee."

"Can anybody sneak in?"

"If there are heartbeats and no aerosol tag, a security breach system is activated. It is very effective. In general, tenants and Wallace Images staffs do not know about the tracking systems."

Roy took the counter clockwise direction in the corridor. Mark followed until they arrived at a small model of the earth hovering below the ceiling. Roy turned as if ready to walk into the room and the door panel slid open.

There were several small work tables in back of the room, some recliners and a refreshment bar. The front of the room was all glass that looked into a cubic-shaped room fifty feet on a side. It was empty. The walls were white. The outlines for the viewing windows for the other rooms surrounding the cube were visible. Three of the windows were transparent and people could be seen inside. In front of the window was a low, slightly inclined console with several computer monitors, keyboards, and rows of levers in slots, and buttons.

"It looks like a combination music mixing studio and an Atari game controller," Mark said.

"All of the above and then some. Another team is running. They have fifteen more minutes."

"I don't see anything."

"They must be entering a new set of data. The re-fresh is slow, depending on the resolution and level of complexity."

An aerial model of the earth suddenly appeared. It was twenty feet in diameter and Florida was in front of the window. The eye of the storm was three hundred miles east of the South Carolina and Florida border. A still pattern of swirling clouds stretched across Florida. The still pattern jumped to life and the hurricane eye moved north and west toward the coast. It arched north and east, and moved further east out into the Atlantic.

"Looks like they won't have to evacuate," Roy said.

"Is this where the television weather models are generated?"

"No. It could be used for that. The people in the room next to us are checking to see if the anticipated volcano eruption in Mexico tomorrow will emit enough matter into the upper atmosphere to affect the energy and path of the hurricane."

"Who are these guys?"

"They are part of a Wallace Images Research Fellow Program.

"The staff here at Wallace Images thought that the developments in three-dimensional modeling might be combined with stochastic diffusion processing of historical events. Research grants had been awarded to two resident-scientists and a scientist from industry, one from the military, one from a university and an artist. Their interest is high atmosphere pollution."

"The research has focused on the time frame 1890 to 2003 with projections to 2015 and beyond, with varying degrees of confidence. Data input to the model included industrial pollutant by-products, which are discharged directly into the air or that provided the catalytic process resulting in airborne pollutants. Data also included solid waste processing by-products that affected air quality directly or indirectly. Data on pollutants that impacted ocean processes that mediated air quality was included in the models. Rain forest degradation, satellite and space probe debris and nuclear testing discharges have been input into the models."

"The evolving system was providing highly accurate forecasts on El Niño and La Niña and a better historical fit with past observations than other computer models. Tectonic, seismology and vulcanology data was input into the model and fit to historical atmospheric events and weather patterns. Atmospheric changes, ice age patterns, and polar shift data were part of the 'archive' data but not emphasized in current prediction models. Satellite data and other sensors were direct inputs to the model. Pending volcano activity and nuclear tests were used to make forecasts and compared with actual outcomes."

"There is an expected eruption tomorrow in central Mexico. They are looking at what happens to the hurri-cane for different amounts of airborne material. When the eruption occurs they will get some idea which of their modeling procedures works best."

"Wow." Mark said as the globe disappeared.

"They are done. We can have WIGS for awhile." Roy keyed in some commands on the computer in front of him and the globe reappeared like a giant atlas. "We are fifty miles up with this view and can zoom in anywhere you want. Do you want to see cities?" He hit a couple of keys and the WIGS blinked as the image cleared and reappeared with what appeared to be cities. "Zoom in on Manhattan on a local screen," Roy said, as the computer monitor in front of Mark displayed a view of an expanding city.

"It looks like entering Manhattan from outer space."

"Central Park."

Mark's console zoomed in on Central Park with a view comparable with that from a helicopter over the city.

"How tight a shot can you get?"

"As tight as technology and clearance will allow," Roy said. "What you are looking at isn't much more than a static city map with known buildings rendering. Fractals are used to add texture. You can get the same thing in your car navigation system. It is possible with a couple more buttons to tap into satellite data and actually zoom in on somebody walking across the street. But enough of the gee-whiz stuff. Let's look at your problem. Where do we want to go?"

"South and east of Aconcagua."

"Southern Chile, here we come."

"You can see the glaciers. Wait a minute, Roy, I don't want anyone else in on this."

"No problem." Roy pushed a button labeled SECURE and the viewing window all around the inside of the WIGS room closed.

"First let me show you how to navigate on WIGS. It needs to know what you are looking at. You can specify coordinates by keying them in on your keyboard, or select with a mouse, or have WIGS use retinal direction. It will track what you are looking at."

"Like pilots looking at instruments?"

"Same technology. First hit the VC button. It stands for Visual Calibration. Four colored spots will appear several times. As each spot appears, look at it and press the VC button. Okay do it for as long as spots appear."

Mark pressed the VC button and a white disk appeared. He pressed the VC button. A red disk appeared followed by a white one, a green one, a red one, an orange one, a blue one, a yellow one and a black one. The word "Calibrated" flashed three times where the spots had appeared.

Roy explained that the colors represented different altitudes.

"Besides depth you can specify the area, that is, you can zoom in and out pretty much the same way you would with a computer mouse. Your eye is the cursor. You have to press these buttons to indicate zoom direction or to mark the area to be expanded."

Mark looked at the general area of Aconcagua, the highest peak in South America and the Western Hemisphere. He held down the zoom in button. As the image of the mountain got larger he kept looking at the summit. The summit centered on the monitor. As he got closer to the summit the surrounding countryside slid off the edges of the monitor.

"How far can I go down?"

"Probably farther than you think. You can zoom down to the last layer of data available. That will be the last recorded satellite shot of the summit and possibly a subterranean layer based on known geologic structure including fractal-generated extrapolations of core sampling. If you had a drilling rig on top of Aconcagua, drilled down a thousand feet and put that data into WIGS, then you could zoom in a thousand feet."

"You mean we could put all our coring data into WIGS?"

"See what a good salesman I am? You can become a WIGS customer." Roy smiled. "For you a deal," and laughed.

"One more razzle and dazzle and then we can get back to your problem." Roy pointed to a button labeled "PEEL" and said, "This is where your geological exploration can get fun. Peel is kind of like zoom in but instead of reducing the field of view it peels away a layer; it goes deeper. If you dropped a box into a lake you could stay with the sinking box by peeling away the water above."

"Can you combine peeling and zooming in?"

"Sure. Okay, now that you know how to navigate, show me where your problem is."

"Probably the best way is to follow the route the helicopters took." Mark pressed the zoom-out button until he could see the Antarctic and Aconcagua on the same screen. Then he looked east to Punta Alta, a small town in Brazil on the Bahia Blanca on the Atlantic. "We have a small drilling operation here in a village near Punta Alta."

"Each pilot followed the Colorado River to the Salado tributary. Then up the Salado to the Tunuyan and then followed the Tunuyan to its headwaters." A small circle on the screen showed where his eyes focused. He zoomed in and out.

At the northern most point of the Tunuyan his eyes strayed up to Mendoza. He zoomed in on the town and then into the streets. Mark tapped the screen at one spot and said, "There is a great little restaurant here."

"Check the menu. See what today's special is."

"Can we do that?"

"Only in surveillance mode. Now we are at static data."

Mark returned to the headwaters of the Tunuyan. "We entered a plateau up here." The aerial view showed a number of deep, winding canyons. "It reminds me of the Grand Canyon in Arizona. You drive along on this flat plateau and suddenly there is a cliff that drops off to nowhere."

"Hit the button labeled 'Geology,'" Roy said.

A floating window appeared indicating that the first two thousand feet consisted of lava flows. There was an indication of several major deposits over a period of two million years. A small comment on the bottom of the window noted that the data was an extrapolation.

"Hit 'Geology' again."

Mark responded and the window disappeared.

"Based on GPS coordinates this is where the first helicopter went into a canyon. He zoomed in and went to the bottom of the canyon."

"We are only looking at fractal creations of the walls."

"Can we go into the surveillance mode?" Mark asked.

"It will take a second or two." Roy pushed buttons and a slightly different view appeared. This was a satellite view. The boundaries were not as well defined as those on maps.

"I'm having a problem zooming into the canyon," Mark said.

"I see. The satellites we are using are commercial grade. They don't provide the polar coverage we need and don't have the resolution. Let's tap into some private satellites." Roy picked up a phone and punched in a number, an access code. "Graham. Can I have access to camera 23? Five minutes. Thanks." He punched in another sequence of data.

"In five minutes we should get a call indicating we can pick fleas off a monkey at the bottom of your canyon. We should also be able to do an infrared and metal resonance survey."

Roy went to the refreshment counter and poured a cup of coffee. The small refrigerator had cream, milk, and three brands of cola. "Want something?"

"Coffee smells good. I'd like to crack open a bottle of Champagne or something. What I've seen blows my mind. How do we get one?" He walked over to Roy and accepted the cup of coffee. "Black, thanks."

"We'll talk about that later." Roy returned to his chair facing WIGS. The phone rang.

"The resolution is fantastic. The image must be an order of magnitude sharper than what we saw a few minutes ago." Mark laughed as he zoomed in on a leaf on the edge of the canyon and watched a leaf cutter ant carrying a piece of leaf down a vine. "This is unbelievable."

"Okay," Roy said,"Start your climb into the valley. If there are three helicopters and fourteen bodies we should find something."

They peered into the canyon and up and down the walls for ten minutes.

"Nothing. Are we in the right canyon?" Roy looked at Mark with a puzzled look. "Let's jump over to the next one."

Another twenty minutes passed as they scanned up and down the walls in several canyons before the phone rang.

Roy answered. "Thank you," and punched in a sequence of numbers.

"Log off security. We have been bumped. I don't think we would have found anything more in twenty or thirty minutes anyway."

"I agree."

"Did you see anything unusual?" Roy looked at Mark.

Mark shook his head. "There didn't seem to be much animal life but I'm not sure what should be there.

There were some unusual rock fragments in the bottom of two of the canyons. They looked more like broken, river-worn granite than basalt."

"I saw those. A couple pieces look like they had holes drilled in them."

"Looks like GOD is playing more tricks on geologists, or somebody is down there or has been down there."

"Is, I think. The fractures looked new." Roy stared at WIGS and punched the OFF button. "There are a couple of problems here. One is what happened to your choppers. The other is, if they were intervened, where is all the evidence? Is the ability to hide something like this a security problem?"

"I know what you are suggesting but I would like to keep the military out of this until GOE covers its tail."

"Understood. There is another approach."

"You mean other than going in by foot?"

"Yes, but it is probably too risky. Send in another chopper and we watch what happens to it from here."

"I'm not sure Lars would want to lose another chopper and put another crew at risk."

CHAPTER 4
HOODS

Roy and Mark return to Roy's place, an old fire station on Capital Hill that served as home, office and warehouse. Their intent was to organize a foot party to approach the canyons from the lower end.

Before they left WIGS Roy had switched to static mode and printed maps of the region of interest from the available data. "This will not be easy." He spread out the maps. "The data is sparse. It's rugged and remote. There are no roads anywhere. The only travel is by foot and air. We will be entering from Argentina. You already have operations there, in Punta Alta."

"Right."

"Can you think of any problems we might have in getting permission to explore the upper reaches of the Tunuyan?"

"If we are surveying we need permits. I am not sure we can tell them we were already there and lost a helicopter, or two."

"Maybe you were taking a business trip to Santiago. It is just the other side of the border. Your helicopter didn't show up. Now you want to go look for it."

"Why would we go by foot then? If we were concerned we would do an aerial survey. Also, we should have filed a flight plan."

"Maybe Lars could work through diplomatic channels and indicate what has happened. Find out if you inadvertently wandered into a secure military area where cooperation would be better than a lot of publicity."

"That would sound like a threat and we can't afford government retaliation. Besides, once a question gets asked it bounces around a lot. GOE, like any other exploration company, doesn't like others to know where they are looking. If word got out we were interested in the upper Tunuyan, every major exploration company would swarm the place."

Mark looked at a map. "We need a story as to why we are going in on foot."

"We could be anthropologists, tourists, adventurers looking for a new river to kayak. Anything but geologists for an oil or mineral exploration company."

"The stone fragments we saw might interest an anthropologist. Would an exploration company ever provide transportation, say, for hire or support to academic scientific projects?"

"Okay, Roy, let's say your adventure company is looking for a site for a management team building experience. You already have credentials for that. Your practice is to review possible sites with an anthropologist, geologist and botanist to prepare educational and orientation materials for your clients."

"That could work. You can be the geologist. We will connect you to a university and avoid GOE identification. Let me see if one of the RENGCA group would be interested in going as the anthropologists. We need a botanist."

"GOE has a couple of guys who know their plants. We do a lot of bio surveying. The minerals in the ground influence plant growth. Horace Bronson is good. His fiancée was the DNAS operator on the first chopper that disappeared."

"Also, we will need a couple of guides who speak English, Spanish and the local dialect. Can you have your office in Punta Alta find somebody? We might want to get some porters from a village downstream to help carry equipment up to the entrance into the canyons. They could walk back to their village."

"Are we rafting or kayaking?"

"Rafting. Actually, we really won't know until we know more about the river. If we find somebody, rafts will be better for transporting. I will have Juan come up with a shopping list for a rafting trip for ten to twelve."

"How about weapons?"

"Juan has never been part of anything other than the adventure trips. Communications, security, weapons and transportation from Punta Alta will be your department. I will talk to RENGCA."

"Sounds like we have a plan. Let me get back to McGurdo Bay. I'll fly commercial to Buenos Aires and have someone pick me up. It's a two-hour jet helicopter ride to Punta Alta from there. Horace is stationed in Punta Alta. I'll brief him and have him find guides while I get back to the ice house."

Roy and Mark spent the rest of the evening making lists of items for Juan and deciding which canyon entrances they would travel to.

In the morning Roy drove Mark to Sea-Tac airport. "This damn place is under constant renovation," Roy commented. "I guess they will keep expanding runways and parking lots until the last tree in the Pacific Northwest is cut down."

The curb area outside Mark's airline was lined with cars so Roy had to stop in the second lane away from the curb. Mark shook Roy's hand and climbed out. "I'll be in Punta Alta tonight and on the ice tomorrow night. I'll call you from there. Goodbye, Sir."

"No 'Sir' on this trip."

"Understood, Roy, old buddy."

Roy drove back to Seattle and to Magnolia Bluff, past the totem pole and past the protestors. Before he was at the gate he said "ROY" and the gate opened. The sensors at the security station detected the voice print vibration from the windshield.

At the hand pad identifier he pushed harder with his little finger to indicate he was going to his office. No images appeared over the door of an elevator that appeared as he approached the paneled scene of a forest.

"Max, I need to talk with you." He said and pressed the "End" button on the intercom. He walked to the refreshment bar for a cup of coffee then to a wall-sized display panel of the Tunuyan. "Target," he said, and a red spot appeared on the panel where he was focusing. "Expand." A red circle appeared and expanded slowly. "Stop." The circle enclosed the northern portion of the Tunuyan down to the junction of the Tunuyan and the Salado.

There was a light knock on the door and Maximillian Schnell, the RENGCA Facilitator at Wallace Images, entered. "Great map. I've seen more detail on a map of the Sahara desert."

"It is sparse isn't it? I think in the next few weeks there will be a few data layers added." Roy became more emphatic, "Max, somewhere in here three helicopters belonging to a friend disappeared." The area with the circle changed color as he spoke. "Mark Stark, whom you will probably meet in the future and I looked into these canyons with satellite linkage. We found nothing of the choppers. However we did find these."

A picture of a red sandy dry riverbed appeared on the panel. In one corner were several lighter colored rocks. Two looked like fragments of a broken rock. Down the center of one of the broken surfaces was a groove.

"This groove looks like what is left of a hole that was drilled in this rock." Roy was circling the two pieces with his right index finger. "Capture." A printed photo version of the area he had just circled slid out of the panel in front of him. He handed it to Maximillian. They walked over to the waist-high drafting table Roy used for a work surface.

Maximillian studied the photo. "This groove looks like it has been drilled but it's very irregular. I've seen some old Native American jewelry where turquoise was drilled with a diamond or other hard mineral on the end of a twist stick. Like starting a fire with a bow and stick. Primitive but effective."

"This rock didn't come from the local matrix."

"That is not unusual. Rocks get carried by rivers long distances. If this was drilled it was probably carried by a person or maybe on an animal that ran away. Say a mule or alpaca carrying the rock ran away and fell off a cliff. That could break the rock. Maybe someone put the rock in a condor nest after stealing an egg to fool the bird. The bird finds the rock, carries it up and drops it. It lands on another rock and breaks along the line of the hole. Stranger things have happened. Maybe…"

"I got the point Max," Roy cut Maximillian off. "Just because we find an isolated broken rock where three helicopters should be doesn't necessarily mean people might be involved."

"Aha. You called me because you have a problem involving Stone Age technology winning over modern technology." Maximillian smiled. "Seagulls cause jets to crash if they are sucked into an air inlet."

"Yes but seagull shit doesn't have holes in it. Max, who lives in that area? Do you have anyone who knows the area that might be interested in going on a little field trip? It might be dangerous."

"Enrique Salivare is our expert on South America." Max said the name again followed by a "Show" command. Enrique's picture and biography appeared on the monitor in front of Roy. "He does have field experience in the Amazon and in the Andes near Machu Picchu but not as far south as Aconcagua. He has been gathering some data on ancient sites below your area, however, closer to Santa Cruz and Tierra del Fuego. If he could find people using Stone Age technology farther North I think he would jump at the chance to go."

"He and several others are developing some simulations of how civilization migrated. He is the person with primary responsibility for South America."

"Elmira Cohen," Maximillian added the command "SHOW". "She is with a museum in Israel and here she is responsible for African migrations. She speaks seven languages and wants to do field work. Although she works the museum, she is tough and could do field work. She was in the Israeli infantry..." A picture of her in military garb appeared. "...before she went to school in languages and ancient and modern technology migration. She is better with technology based artifacts than Henry, I mean Enrique.

"The only other person who is on site is Achmed Rahim. He is our resident Muslim and is the coordinator for India."

"Sounds like Enrique is a logical choice for this," Roy said. "But you decide. Be sure to consider yourself a candidate."

"I'm out. I get nosebleeds above fifteen thousand. I'll talk to the others and get back to you later this afternoon."

"Thanks, Max."

Maximillian left the office. Roy picked up the phone and keyed in a number. He wasn't aware of a ring at the other end but a lady answered.

Roy, "George, please."

"Is General Parker your call?"

"Always."

"Who shall I say is calling?"

"Maggie, cut out the formal stuff."

"Yes, Roy. Are you coming out? It has been a long, long time."

"Roy, good to hear from you. What kind of crazy trips you planning now? I had to pull you from the drink on the last one."

"My mortal being will forever be grateful. George, I am in fact organizing a small reconnaissance trip. Something has come up that might be of concern to you. Mark Sharp has lost three choppers in a remote area. We used satellite twenty-three cameras and scoured every inch of the target area with no signs."

"I noticed you used my eyes in the sky. Not too many people outside this office know about it."

"Right."

"How is Mark? I haven't heard from him since when-ever. It has been a long time. What is the concern?"

"At the target we did find evidence of possible habitation. Stone age habitation."

"You mean somebody threw rocks at choppers and brought them down?

"Three of them and left no trace. Anybody that can do that should be a concern."

"I agree. What do you need?"

"Can you have the target monitored for a couple of days? Take shots every fifteen minutes. Get visual, infrared, metal resonance. If there are any perturbations increase the snap rate as needed."

"I think we can do that."

"Thanks."

Two days later Roy was jogging along a virtual reality, rock and boulder-strewn mountain trail. The atmosphere in the room holding the flexible moving belt that would distort to simulate obstacles was filtered to reduce oxygen and depressurized to lower the relative vapor pressure in order to simulate higher altitudes. He was starting to acclimatize his body to the higher elevations he would be going to in the southern Andes.

A soft voice said, "Phone." While he ran he answered, "Roy."

"Your birds have been found. Check their cages."

The communication ended.

"Good old General Parker," Roy thought. "END," he said. The belt flattened and slowed down and the scenery disappeared.

Still sweating, he jogged to his office. "IN BOX," he said as he entered the room. "DISPLAY." The panel he and Mark had looked at displayed the upper Tunuyan basin and one hundred miles south of the canyons flashed a red circle. He reached toward the display and a photo of a pile of steel, magnesium, titanium, carbon fiber and Plexiglas scraps slid into his hand. A second photo appeared that showed that each piece of scrap was stained with brown matter and yellow dye. Four skulls could be seen scattered in the wreckage.

A third photo appeared with text. "In addition to satellite Twenty-three observations, a commercial pilot flying from Buenos Aires to Santiago had detoured south to avoid a large thunderstorm and saw reflections from what appeared to be metal. At first he thought someone was sending a distress signal with a mirror. He circled lower and saw the wreckage which he reported when arriving in Santiago. It is assumed that either the Chilean or Argentine air force or both will be investigating."

Roy calls Mark. "Good news, your choppers have been found. Bad news, the local air forces will probably get there. You have to bite the bullet, tell them they are your choppers, and send somebody there before the locals do. More bad news: Body parts."

Mark indicates there were highly industrially sensitive devices on board the first and third choppers that even the military doesn't know about. "Roy, we can't afford for this technology to get out."

"Nuclear, biological, what?"

"None of that. Nothing harmful that would pose a risk to the environment or people physically. The way the world works it could represent the ultimate surveillance device. Can you get Parker to put a cover over it."

"Probably but the product would have to be classified and put into Pandora's Box. I'm sure GOE can continue to work with it but under constraints. You know the drill."

"What is the technology?"

"I can't explain here. Remember your birthday present? It was analyzed from the air?"

"No way."

"Believe me."

"Okay, make the assumption that you are covered. Get your ass up there in a big hurry. Your fax should have the photo."

"I see it. How did the parts get way over there?"

"Did you give me the right coordinates to begin with?"

"Absolutely."

"Is there any magnetic anomaly or other force that could interrupt GPS transmission?"

"Not that I know of. Roy, are you coming down?"

"No, there is too much to do here. You get up there and cordon off the area and do a forensic sweep. I'll arrange for a clean-up crew to secure everything as long as we can get there first."

Roy called General Parker's office. "Hi, Maggie. Twice in a decade. Interrupt him then."

"Something for your box, if you hurry."

"Great what is it?"

"Can't tell you now. Here is what we need however." Roy explained the need for immediate diplomatic intervention, and securing of the site and materials.

"I saw the wreckage and figured you would want something to happen so coverage was underway. A new toy will be a bonus."

Four airborne warships were being prepared to leave Santa Clara, a small island west of Chile on a parallel with Santiago as Roy was on the phone. Mark was on a Mach Three VTOL. It would still take him over two hours to reach the site. The Chilean air force command was preparing to do a fly-over reconnaissance before sending in a high altitude helicopter. They expected to be on the plateau in two hours. The Argentine Air Force would be delayed in getting a helicopter ready and would have a four-hour arrival time. The Argentineans were suggesting to the Chileans that the sighting was in Argentina and the Chilean fly-over would be frowned upon. Neither was enthusiastic about the American intervention.

The race to the wreckage resulted in a partial stand-off. The craft on the scene was a Chilean helicopter with a pilot and co-pilot. They landed fifty feet from the pile of metal. Some of the lighter parts blew off the top and dust blew into the pile.

"The first gun ship coming in from the West saw the Chilean craft on the ground. The Chilean pilot was climbing out of the cockpit and walking toward the pile. At the same time when the gun ship pilot first saw the wreckage site he saw some animals loping away from the area. "What are those?" The co-pilot shook his head.

The gun ship circled around and was positioned on the opposite side of the metal heap down wind from the Chilean pilot. The front guns swiveled and pointed at him. The Chilean pilot gave the pilot of the gun ship the finger.

The draft from the gun ship blew dust in the direction of the pile. There was a foul odor the Chilean pilot had not noticed upwind when he landed. The blast of air from the gun ship reached him. He staggered and grasped his mouth and nose. Stumbling backward holding his nose he said, "Mapinguari!" and returned to his helicopter.

The pilot in the gun ship had a directional voice amplifier focused on the pilot, expecting to have a conversation with him about leaving the area. "What did he say?"

The American co-pilot said, "I think the local translation is bad smell, or very bad odor."

The Chilean co-pilot was halfway to the wreckage and stopped when the Americans landed and his pilot ran back to the helicopter.

A figure emerged from the gun ship, dressed in black, pointing a gun at the Chilean. He approached the pile and suddenly turned away and knelt down. Several guns could be heard clicking into a ready mode. He signaled that everything was okay and put on a gas mask.

As he walked around the pile to the Chilean co-pilot and got upwind he noticed what appeared to be feces and urine markings on all the parts.

"Bad omen," The Chilean said looking at the American who had taken off his gas mask.

The remaining three gun ships arrived and landed below the first. Each pointed in a different direction so that the four had their nose guns pointing to the four directions of the compass.

Mark's helicopter arrived and landed west of the Chilean. Mark had been warned about odor and emerged with his gas mask on.

The pieces had been dismantled by being chopped up and pulverized by blunt and sharp instruments. There were no metal tool marks. It looked like the choppers had been cut up with sharp rocks. Some pieces were broken cleanly as if the metal had fatigued and simply cracked apart. A quick attempt at locating fingerprints was futile. There was some form of paw or pad marks, like fingers without fingerprints or gloves. There was blood on a number of pieces.

Mark went to his helicopter and returned with a DNA Scintillator. He pressed the switch below the DNAS label. The commandos at the site did not turn their heads and look directly at the strange device but they looked out of the corners of their eyes. There was a flurry of imperceptible body gestures. One commando pointed his chin slightly, another lifted his shoulders a fraction of an inch, and another turned his head to the left about three degrees and back. They had been told that a classified item would be used that was never to be discussed.

Mark scanned the blood on the wreckage with DNAS and identified DNA from 10 people that were missing. Traces of skin identified two more.

There were four human skulls that looked like they had been boiled and the contents scooped out. Gold fillings from two skulls had been knocked out. DNA from two skulls matched blood found on the wreckage. The other two accounted for the rest of the fourteen lost crew.

There were traces of skin and fur that did not register on DNAS. They would be taken to Wallace Images for study along with samples of the feces and scraping of the urine stains. All materials would be photographed and transferred to a secured hanger at McChord Air Force Base. There a thorough forensic analysis would be made. Roy had indicated he wanted to know where the parts had been. He wanted to know the origin of every speck of dust, every pollen particle, every drop of blood.

Mark noticed ten hooded figures in the distance watching. In his binoculars he saw they wore a hooded robe that hid their faces. The robes appeared to be of roughly twisted cord of hemp or fur. No part of their hands, feet or face could be seen.

"Who are they?" he asked the Chilean co-pilot who had stayed back from the wreckage.

"We have a word that is difficult to translate. Some say they are 'Holimen.'" Others say 'Forbidden,' 'Outcasts,' 'Diseased Ones,' or the 'Deformed.' They wander the mountains on a continuous pilgrimage."

Mark called to the American pilot to get a fix on the hooded figures as he looked back in their direction. They were gone! "Did you get them?"

"No," the speaker from the helicopter said. "Either I didn't get there soon enough or they didn't register on the IR sensors. Strange."

Roy met Mark at McChord Air Force Base. "I'm glad you could pick me up here, Roy. I didn't want to explain bottles of strange feces to Customs. I identified all the people we lost from their DNA on parts or in skin or bone fragments."

"I think you are going to have to fill me in on what is going on."

"The short version is this. The DNAS, which is in the back seat, is a Buck Rogers device we developed to enhance our oil exploration efforts. DNAS stands for DNA Scintillator. We program in a DNA pattern in a format we developed. We aim at an object like an animal, or a person, or a fossil and press the trigger. It is basically a combination magnetic field, ultrasonic beam and neutrino field. If the DNA pattern in the object matches that of DNAS the DNA will resonate and absorb energy. When the field is removed the energized DNA radiates the excess energy and returns to its original state. The radiation appears as scintillation on the DNAS screen."

"You mean the police can get a sample of a perpetrator's DNA and fly around looking for scintillation on the screen?"

"Right. That was what the third chopper was doing. Looking for DNA from the previous two."

"Let's avoid mentioning DNAS to GENXPLR."

"Who are they again?"

"One of the Wallace Images tenants. They probably have the world's most complete collection of DNA, or at least have access to it. All kinds of DNA. They have a research effort on DNA regression in addition to the development of a global DNA database and laboratory services for the criminal justice system. They are still using in-the-lab typing. I am not sure what they would do with the DNAS."

"Here we are. Let's drop off the samples with Laney at GENXPLR and go get lunch. Maybe he can have something for us when we get back. Actually, he will give you a dog and pony show first. In the meantime, put the DNAS in the vault in my office."

Laney Smith was a short well-dressed Englishman. He had a big smile when Roy entered and effusively greeted

Mark like a long lost brother. "I cannot imagine living under ice the way you do. I need my lab and the amenities of life." Oxford trained in biology, Masters in biochemistry from MIT and Ph.D. in Genetic Engineering from Caltech, he also did post-graduate work at the Sanger Centre. Laney considered the basic amenities of life to be bigger computers, good wine and good food.

"You have a most interesting collection of specimens but to truly appreciate them you need to know something about what we do."

Mark looked at Roy who cocked his head to one side, shrugged and smiled.

"We do the mundane DNA typing for the authorities. That helps pay the bills. We work with several organizations: DeCode in Iceland, Sanger Centre in Cambridge, Celera Genomics in Rockville Maryland, Affymetrix in Silicon Valley, cataloguing and storing DNA information associated with the gene structures of people. The data is useful in identifying members of families. The Mormons, Catholic Church, and royal families with long recorded lineages from around the world were the starting point. There are some groups of people that have been relatively isolated for a long time, a number of generations like the residents of Iceland and at times a "lost" tribe like the Korubu in Brazil, or the Liawep Tribe in Papua, New Guinea.

"It was necessary to have records of what might have affected genetic transfer. When you get into countries that have suffered wave after wave of war and rape and occupation by different groups, generation after generation, the gene pool sort of levels out. The average gene pool is the real social melting pot. From a pragmatic, long-term survival of the species point of view, that might be good. I doubt, however, the courts will give a rapist any credit for increasing the chances of survival of the human race. With society as crazy as it is, a good lawyer will probably get another slime ball off the hook with the idea."

"Sometimes we just tell WIGS to do its thing and find all the patterns it can that suggest genetic associations. Some strange ideas come up from time to time. WIGS also has a GENEBOT, a program that constantly patrols the web looking for new articles and citations about DNA, Genes and Genomes. Every morning there is a printout of new research articles, jokes, proposed legislation, advertisements for genetically engineered beauty creams and erection dysfunction cures.

Our favorite project, which by the way doesn't pay the rent, is to figure out what the original DNA was that led to the rise of man. Where did we come from?"

Laney Smith looked at Mark and smiled and paused.

"Now," he said. "Let's look at your samples. The urine and feces came from the same entities. I use the plural because there would be too much for one entity, based on what I have been told.

"First, it doesn't seem to be human. At least not quite human. Second, we haven't a clue as to what it is. It has a number of primate characteristics. It is interesting."

"If an object startled a monkey," Mark asked, "and then didn't move, would the monkey make a domination gesture like defecating or urinating on it. Or mark it as a possession?"

"Very possible, very possible." Laney looked excited, like it was the beginning of a new game. "But that only gives us one possible explanation of why it was marked, and nothing about who marked it."

Roy asked, "Every piece was marked with both feces and urine, is that right?"

"Laney, the ten samples that Mark gave you, were they all the same?"

"No. Mark gave me twenty vials labeled F1,U1,F2,U2 and so on. "F" I took to mean feces and "U" urine. The number corresponded to the sample number."

"That's right," Mark nodded.

"The urine and feces for each sample had the same DNA and genome structure, the genome being a collection of DNA molecules with a given pattern. Two of the samples matched exactly. The other eight samples had unique patterns."

Laney was clearly anxious to get back to his findings. "As I suggested, the DNA was not quite human but it had some patterns we find in human groups."

Laney pressed a WIGS button on his desk and his wall display panel showed South America, Central America, Mexico and California. "We did find a sub-pattern that was common to your sample and DNA patterns from two South and Central American groups and one group of Native American Indians in Northern California. What is interesting about this is that there are genomic similarities between tribes that have the same religious and language base. In a small area in Northern California there are three indigenous groups, separated by mountains, and they have three language and religion bases. It seems to raise questions as to where the three groups came from or what path they took. They might not have come across the Bering Strait as we are told in school."

"I have saved the best for last." Laney stood and walked around the room while he talked. "One effort that we have just started involves tracking genome changes over long periods of time. DNA from mummies, museum pieces, old known burial sites, old gravesites unearthed by a bulldozer during a construction process, some court sanctioned grave robbing. We only need a small trace. There is never desecration. I don't want Tribal councils storming the gate outside."

"We have found some, for want of a better term, linear progressions in the change in portions of DNA over time. People have been getting bigger and so forth.

"We asked ourselves the obvious question. If there is a linear relation forward can we extrapolate backwards? The assumption being that mutation from whatever source does not dominate. We call this DNA regression."

"We also run simulations in which we introduce a mutation in DNA locations we know to be critical for defining certain human characteristics. Some of the staff are initiating a Monte-Carlo regression simulation. They will identify the probability of different mutations as part of the model structure and run the simulation a large number of times, say one thousand. Each time the simulation is run the mutation probability tables are sampled and the DNA patterns are changed. Since heredity is primarily a function of mitochondrial DNA we only have to introduce changes there. A DNA composite will be constructed from all the samples. If we change the probability table we again have to run the sampling a thousand times. The work is scheduled for low usage periods on WIGS, which is getting harder to find."

"Gentlemen, there is the suggestion of a possible match with some of our regressed DNA and your samples."

Laney smiled for a long time with his fingertips together in front of him. He wanted to make sure Mark and Roy understood.

"You have found the missing link. Please bring one back."

Mark looked at Roy and stood and shook Laney's hand. "Thank you for your overview and analysis, Dr. Smith. We will try."

Back in Roy's Office, Mark looked at Roy. "Are these guys for real? I want to find out who killed my crew and he wants to find the missing link."

"Mark, old boy. Keep a stiff upper lip, an open mind and all that. You do have to admit that there is something strange going on."

"You are right. Are we ready to take a hike in the woods?"

CHAPTER 5
CAVES

Juan bought three rafts, pack boards onto which they could tie canoe bags, butane stoves, pots, cups, light sleeping bags, insect repellant, dehydrated meals, ropes and anything else he could think of. "We can always give away stuff we don't need," Juan said when Mark looked surprised at the size of the growing pile of equipment in his office.

Roy and Mark met Maximillian Schnell in Schnell's Office. Maximillian called Enrique's intercom. "They are here," he said, "come on over."

Enrique had the barrel-chested, stocky build of a highlander from the Northern Andes. "I am honored being considered for your journey," he said. "I know the mountains and some rivers."

Roy reviewed the basics of the situation. Three helicopters have been lost in a remote region shown on the panel. Satellite photos indicate some rock artifacts of possible interest. Because of the loss of aircraft they thought it prudent to explore on foot from below the canyons in question. The trip was likely to be dangerous.

Enrique said, "Call me Henry. I understand danger and look forward to getting started. I will study the site."

As Roy was standing to leave, the door burst open. The panel instantly blanked out. Elmira Cohen, the African specialist from the Israel Museum of Archaeology, walked with her arms to her sides and fist clenched. She walked straight to Maximillian and when six inches from him she hissed, "What is this macho bullshit? You know I was next in line for a field work assignment. I know more about technology than Walks From Clouds Hank here will ever know. You know I needed this trip to get data for my dissertation."

Roy thought he might diffuse the tension, "What is your dissertation on?"

"Comparative analysis of indigenous technologies between South American and African cultures. Why do you give a shit, whoever you are."

"Elmira, I think you owe Mr. Graham an apology. If it weren't for him, you, and I for that matter, probably wouldn't even be here at Wallace Images."

She looked at Roy stone-faced and left.

Roy suggested that she was very intent in her work and really didn't like getting passed over. "Henry," he said, "glad you can make it. Go to my place, Max can give you directions. Talk to Juan about equipment you will need. He will fix you up with tickets, schedule and all that. He is expecting you. We leave tomorrow night for Buenos Aires. Juan can help you expedite shots and a passport if necessary. See you tomorrow night."

The commercial flight to Buenos Aires was smooth. Everyone slept except for meal breaks. After one break, Juan went to the restroom. Henry moved over and sat in his seat next to Roy.

"Excuse me a minute. I looked up culture in the area and found some interesting notes on a religious preserve. On a map drawn in 1895 there was a dotted line around an area that covers that where we are going. Nothing said about meaning of religious preserve. It seems based on native, what you call, superstitions like Yeti in the Himalayas, Sasquatch in the U.S. or the Yowi in Australia."

"I hadn't heard anything about it," Roy said. "Thank you."

"Mark, did you hear what Henry said?" Roy then noticed Mark was asleep. "I guess we'll tell him in the morning."

In Buenos Aires the equipment was transferred to a GOE helicopter. Horace Bronson, the botanical expert and local manager, had flown from Punta Alta with the pilot to meet them.

Mark hugged Horace. "We are going to do everything we can to find her."

"What's that about?" Roy asked.

"Horace's fiancée was the D." He paused reminded himself not to mention DNAS, "One of the people on the first helicopter that was lost."

Roy asked Mark with a concerned look, "Is he going to be objective if things are not well with her?"

"I hope so. He is our key to getting into the area."

During the flight to Punta Alta Roy sat next to Horace. Horace said, "We'll find something."

Hector Olivera, the GOE local manager in Punta Alta, met them at the airport. He walked them over to the combination Customs office and police station. "We have already made the proper understanding of your trip. The Commandante has heard of the adventures of Mr. Roy Graham and would like to meet him."

"Commandante Bolivar, this is the famous explorer Mr. Roy Graham. He has heard much of you, Commandante, and wanted to meet with you," Hector said with a head bending gesture.

"I understand you are making a rafting trip to bring others, managers and companies here to learn. This is good." He puffed on his cigar and looked Roy in the eyes.

"I am worried a little. Where you go is near a forbidden, dangerous place. You get porters in San Rafael. They will show you. I recommend you not go too far. To do so would not be good."

Two helicopters were packed. The first carrying Juan, Roy and Mark was to fly directly to a basecamp thirty miles past the junction of the Tunuyan and Salado junction fifteen miles below the entrance to the canyons. Horace flew in the other to San Rafael to pick up the four porters Hector had hired.

Roy said, "We know whoever is there can take down a helicopter and dismantle it and transport the parts thirty miles. Let's consider them hostile."

"That's an understatement."

"They didn't take out the chopper above the two hundred-foot level below the rim. We might want a diversion, so lets have a chopper drop to 100 feet and circle around in the canyon we are looking in. If there is somebody there it might provide enough distraction to give us cover."

There was no trail and the river was too rough to use. The team had to break trail in the jungle, over cliffs and rough terrain. It took two days to go ten miles. On the morning of the third day Roy said the GPS readings indicated they were at the openings to the canyons, a small lake fed by four cliff-lined rivers. Wide meadows surrounding the lake were the result of flooding after storms on the plateau above.

They traveled around the left side. Near the opening to the first river a stench filled the air. Juan said, "Bat shit." Mark thought it smelled more like ammonia.

Tied to the first large tree at the entrance of a waterway, like a scarecrow, was a dark brown robe. The porters dropped to their knees and prayed. They were very agitated and told Horace they were in the forbidden area and could not continue. "Mapinguari," they said and indicated they wanted to return to their village. In the middle of the night they left.

"Are we close enough or should we pack gear farther upstream?" Juan asked. Roy suggested they carry the rafts another four miles to what appeared from the maps to be a flat section of canyon floor below where the choppers were lost. " We will travel faster if we leave the rest of the equipment."

There was an increased level of tension as they moved through brush and trees on the left side of the river within hearing distance of the river. The roar of the river stopped and they moved to the right. A large, smooth eddy swirled clockwise drawing the current upstream past a sandy beach.

"I think the rest of the way is rough water." Roy said. "Juan, you Horace and Henry stay here. If Mark and I have to get out fast it will probably be down the river."

Roy and Juan worked out communications signals. They suspected that Roy would not be able to communicate with a helicopter on top for whatever reason. Roy could relay messages to the choppers through Juan.

Juan called the helicopters they had left four days before and found out one chopper had been crippled. The pilot was killed by the frightened porters. The second helicopter relocated and called for a backup helicopter to go to the top.

Roy and Mark put on wet suits. The river temperature was in the low forties and a person in the river without insulating protection would lose muscle control in four minutes. Severe hypothermia would start in eight minutes.

When they entered the mouth of the canyon they found they had to rock climb around several sets of rapids and at times had to give up the cover of sound that the river provided to move through the woods. In some places they would ride the upstream side of the eddy to the protrusion in the river and climb around.

The gorge widened. "We are at the opening to the valley below where the choppers were lost," Roy whispered. The water was smoother but swift.

A network of overhanging vines blocked their view of the canyon walls. Mark whispered, "Looks like camouflage netting." After going around another bend they could see that there were nets suspended between the canyon walls, blocking a clear view of the sky. A mist filled the air.

Water cascaded from openings in the walls. "Lava tubes," Mark said. "They formed when gases were trapped in lava flows like big bubbles before the flows solidified. They can be tens of miles long. I bet the tubes connect the canyons with the plateau like a subway system."

Around another bend the valley floor flattened. Thirty to forty waterfalls cascaded from the walls. "There must have been a dozen lava flows over the centuries and they all have tubes. There are water spouts up as high as I can see," Roy whispers. " That one above the far end of the valley must be 1500 feet above the valley floor." The cascading water fell through openings in the netting. "Whoever made the nets could cover the Rose Bowl stadium."

The river followed the left wall of a crescent shaped valley. Sand deposits to the right of the river angled slightly up to the base of the sheer cliff that rose two thousand feet without a flaw. Dense grasses and thorny bushes covered the first fifty feet of the sand bar. Cactus and small willows and cottonwoods diffused up the slope to larger trees near the base of the cliff.

Mark pointed up as the sound of a helicopter could be heard on top and further up the canyon. "It is above the location where the helicopters were lost."

Roy nodded and indicated he was trying to contact it. Roy pointed to the netting and then the radio and drew a finger across his throat. The net was blocking the signal. He called Juan downstream and explained the situation.

Mark studied the netting with binoculars. "The nets have been repaired many times. There are layers of them in places. Over there against the left bank there is some hanging in the water. It is in a small back eddy. Maybe we can get a piece and check it out."

Roy suggests he will go through the grass, around the bend and drift into the eddy. "When I leave the eddy I will probably come out downstream fifty yards or so."

Roy and Mark have both covered their faces and wet suits with red smears to blend in with the terrain.

Roy worked his way through the grass around the bend. He slipped into the water and heard a shrilled grunt and a human scream. As he drifted into the swifter part of the stream he could see further up the valley. He had a fleeting glimpse of a dozen people with wooden tools bending over rows in a rough garden. A disfigured person was swinging a whip at someone who had fallen. The others in the group kept their faces down. Just as the current spun him into the eddy and out of view of the garden the figure with the whip turned toward Roy. It did not look human. A foul gagging stench drifted in the air along with the water. Roy struggled to hold his breath as he went under the surface to avoid being seen. The ammonia-like smell burned in his lungs.

He felt the gentle tug of the upstream eddy and let his mouth break the surface. He took a clean breath and swam two yards to the wall beneath the hanging remnant of net. The shoulder of the cliff causing the eddy blocked his view of the garden and possible detection. He tried to cut a piece of net with his knife. It resisted. Roy fumbled with a small utility belt and extracted wire cutters. He snipped away a square foot of net and slipped back into the water. He took a deep breath, submerged and pushed into the swift current. Under the churning surface the blue green-water was filled with white air bubbles. He was tossed and somersaulted three or four times before surfacing on the opposite side of the river and was swept past Mark. He signaled he was coming ashore and for Mark to stay low and covered. Fifty feet below where he first saw Mark he grabbed a branch and pulled himself into a thick growth of reeds. He waited for five minutes before sliding onto the bank and crawled back to Mark.

"If you smell something get the hell out of here."

"Why?"

"Something and I mean something is using humans as slaves in a garden just around the bend. I didn't get a good enough look to see if they were your people."

"What did you get?"

"This stuff is tough. There is metal worked into rope. It looks like gold."

"There is also silver and some old copper wire woven into the hemp and hide strands."

"That's why we can't detect them from the air. They have a gigantic screen room."

"You mean like the screen rooms in the electronic instrument labs. Wire screen around a room keeps outside electro-magnetic signals from getting inside."

"Right."

"But this stuff is so unbelievably primitive."

"But effective. We can't contact the chopper on the ridge."

"We are not blocked from Juan and Horace are we?"

"Try them."

"Juan, Juan, do you copy." Mark inserted a small earpiece and started to whisper into a pencil-sized communicator pointed downstream.

Roy said, "Hold it. Smell that? Slip into the water quietly. Let's drift down past that log."

Surfacing below the log they swam back to the eddy behind it and peered upstream from a two-inch opening under the log. The current waves splashed against the opening, blocking their view every few seconds.

The entity appeared on the shoulder of the bank. It stood four to five feet high. It looked downstream and up the cliffs. A falcon with a rodent in its beak dropped from the cliff and landed on the creature's outstretched arm. The creature grasped the rodent from the bird, bit off the head and sucked the entrails out of the body.

While it chewed and picked in the rodent cavity with a long fingernail, urine sprayed from an erect penis. It looked up the cliff on the other side of the river, turned and casually threw the eviscerated rodent body into the stream. Walking back toward the garden it shoved the falcon into the air. The bird rose in widening circles and disappeared above the netting with a shrill. The creature shrilled back.

"Tell me what you saw." Mark said. "I don't believe what I did."

"It had dark, straggly-hair-covered, spotted hide."

"Check."

"Its legs looked like goat hind legs. I couldn't tell if it had hoofs or feet."

"Check."

"Big slong and gets off on eating."

"Check."

"It has spines or long tuffs of stiff hair every three inches or so down its back."

"Check."

"Its arms were sinewy looking and its hands looked like those of a chameleon. Long fingers with pads on the tips. It had a big thumb. I couldn't tell if it had fingernails or claws."

"Check."

"Its head looked like ET. Big eyes. The nose area reminded me of a bat. The lips covered the teeth when it bit off the head."

"Check."

"So, Mark, what did you see?"

"Same thing you did, a Mapinguari or a distant cousin."

"That is as good a label as any for now."

"Try Juan again."

Mark explained what Roy had seen and problems with communication. "Juan, we need a diversion so we can assess the situation. There are creatures up here that are using people as slaves. They are probably associated with the hooded figures I saw wandering around on top a few days ago. The diversion is going to have to look like a legitimate operation that is going to last a couple of days."

"The crew on top has to be ready to get out of there fast if anything shows up, animals or holimen. If the clouds part and Michael appears to them and says 'behold there will be good tidings,' have them get the hell out of there."

They coordinated a quick fly-by on top.

Roy moved to the bank where he first saw the garden. When he heard the helicopters overhead, a single creature in the garden started to drive the people into a cave. They were all naked or wore rags around their waists. When the last person was hidden a net dropped over the entrance.

The sound of the chopper went away. Ten minutes passed. The net was raised and captives stumbled into the garden. There was only one apparent sentry.

"Juan, have the chopper pilot drop a couple hundred pennies that have been soaked in insect repellent to disguise human smell, and a dozen oranges into the canyon with notes inside indicating Mark is watching and to signal how many guards there are. Exactly ten minutes after they leave the canyon have them fly back a half a mile up the canyon and drop flares."

Three hours later the chopper made another flight. It hovered a hundred feet in the canyon. As the Mapinguari were driving the humans into the cave, pennies and oranges crashed down through the netting. The net covering the cave dropped. Five minutes passed before the Mapinguari cautiously exited the cave. It sniffed and walked to an orange, picked it up, sniffed and nibbled the rind. It spit out the bits of rind and threw the orange away. Sniffing, it picked up a penny and returned to the cave.

Roy handed Mark the binoculars. It doesn't like oranges but does like pennies. They use metal. He will probably send out the people to pick them up. If there is more than one Mapinguari tending the garden, the others might come out.

Ten minutes after the chopper left the rim, the humans were shoved into the garden area by three Mapinguari. One of the three stands with a whip. The other two push people down to a penny and seem to give an instruction to find pennies and bring them to the Mapinguaris.

"Hey, that's John Bartram who just gave the beast a penny. He was co-pilot on the first helicopter.

"Oh my God, Peggy is there. What have they done to her? She is completely naked and smeared with mud except where the whip has left marks."

"That probably is not mud."

"Whoa, Walt Woltowski, the DNAS operator on the third chopper just picked up an orange. He found the note. Damn."

"What."

"The Mapinguari cut him down with a whip. He is alive. I can see him move."

Roy and Mark could hear the whip cracking as the humans shuffled through the garden looking for pennies. If they approached an orange the whip cracked behind them and they moved on.

"Walt," Mark whispered, "just held up three fingers and collapsed."

"Don't even think, just shoot. I'll take the whip and the one on the left. You take the guy on the right. Keep your eye on the tunnel."

The silencers gave a slight pop as three shots were fired. Roy and Mark ran as fast as they could toward the garden. Both held a finger to their lips signaling for everyone to be quiet.

Nobody moved. They stood and looked at Roy and Mark running toward them and cowered. "Into the river."

Mark and Roy pointed to the river and pushed. Nobody wanted to move. Roy picked up the whip and cracked it twice and pointed to the river. Twenty people shuffled stupefied toward the water and hesitated when their feet sank in the wet sand at the edge. Mark had thrown Walt over his shoulders and run toward the river. He knocked five people into the water and threw Walt in. Mark and Roy were grabbing arms and shoving as fast as they could. Peggy turned to Mark, her body smeared with feces and breasts bleeding from a whiplash and stared at him. Tears welled up in his eyes and he pushed her into the river. He pushed two more people into the river and dove in after them.

A falcon swooped down on Roy, talons outstretched, ripped a piece of neoprene from his wet suit, and circled upward to a tunnel high on the cliff wall.

Roy yelled at Mark to key in the emergency signal to Juan. "Let him know we are coming down river like a bunch of drowned rats."

Arms flayed in the air and splashed at the water. Whenever someone tried to crawl out on a rock, or log or the bank, Roy or Mark threw them back in. They were swept through stacks of white water where the current held them under for thirty feet. The river banks narrowed in places to twenty feet across. Heads bobbed up and down and some people just floated face down, arms outstretched at eighteen miles an hour. The river opened to rapids and boulders. Nobody was trying to escape. Hypothermia would be setting in in a few more minutes. Only Roy and Mark were protected from the bone chilling, muscle-numbing cold water at fifteen thousand feet. The banks closed in and swept twenty bodies into another narrow gorge that curved to the right and opened into a wide, placid, smooth flow.

"Boss, we see you." Juan, Henry and Horace waded into the quiet water of an eddy and started dragging bodies onto the bank. The curvature of the narrow gorge forced the water to spin clockwise. When the river widened the water continued its clockwise motion into and along the bank and moved upstream.

Roy and Mark swam to bodies that had floated past the eddy and pulled them into it so they floated upstream against the bank.

"My daddy always said that everything in a river eddies out," said Horace, standing in the water at the edge of the sandy beach. He grunted as he grasped the arm of the last person drifting past the beach face down. Horace fell backwards pulling in the near-dead person.

"If they cough put them on their stomach downhill and get to the next person," Roy said as he, Mark, Horace and Henry were administering artificial respiration to as many people as they could.

Roy shouted to Juan, "Get on the radio. Get the chopper to drop incendiaries where they had dropped the pennies and then downstream for a hundred yards. Then get down here for air cover. We have to put these people into three rafts and get down to the clearing. Tell them we have twenty-four people down here."

Roy watched Mark gently put his palms below Peggy's lacerated breasts. The water had washed the feces off her body. Mark started a sharp forceful cycle of compressions. She coughed. He turned her naked body over and went to the next person. Horace hadn't yet seen her.

Several people were sitting up or on hands and knees. Horace said,"I think there are two we can't help."

"Put them in the bottom of the rafts," Roy said. "I am not going to let them be eaten by those creatures. Pile everybody else in."

A couple of people were able to stagger over to a raft and fall in. Others were carried and fit into an opening. People were moaning "No more. No more."

"Poor souls," Mark said, "They probably think we are just another version of the creatures on top but with ice water."

"There is no guarantee everybody is going to make it."

Roy and Mark pushed the rafts into the current. The rafts picked up momentum and drifted quietly down the river.

Juan asked, "Boss is this the proverbial 'up a river without any paddlers?'" There were eight people in each raft. Only four people could paddle.

"I can help," Walt said feebly. He struggled to push himself against the side of the raft where he could paddle. Over the next ten minutes eight more recovered enough to understand what was happening and started to paddle. Nobody spoke. The only sound was the trickling of water dripping off the paddles and small waves slapping the sides of the rafts. The river slid like silk in a breeze past the steep cliffs.

"Thunk." One of the paddlers in Juan's raft quietly rolled over the edge and started to drift with a spear in his back. Juan grabbed the paddle and handed it to a wide-eyed Indian who spoke no English but understood paddling. There were no war whoops or cries from above.

The rafts rounded a bend. Another spear struck a person in Mark's raft. It went through his thigh and into one of the bodies in the bottom of the raft. Roy saw the creature as the spear was released and shot it. Mark saw another preparing to throw and shot it. When the two dark-skinned creatures hit the water a general panic started in the rafts. Several captives started coarse, monotonic screams and tried to climb out. Roy knocked one person out with a quick punch. Horace did the same. "Stay," Roy screamed. Everyone cowered.

The rafts rounded a bend. The river widened and a bright clearing could be seen below that point. They were at the edge of the preserve where the porters had fled. Lining the top of the forty-foot cliff were fifteen Mapinguaris with spears poised.

"How many shots do you have, Roy?"

"Seven, and you?"

"Three."

The current carried them toward the base of the cliff. A high shrill pierced the air. The Mapinguari raised their spears and started spraying urine. They spread their legs and squatted and raised several times, defecating each time. Their shrilling reached a near-earsplitting pitch.

"Sounds like bats coming out of a cave," Horace sat quietly and started to cross himself. Henry and several others sat up straight, looked at the Mapinguari, and crossed themselves.

The sound of gentle waves slapping against the raft was drowned by the roar of the nose cannons from a flying stealth gunship that emerged from around the edge of the bright meadow. The chilled, traumatized, naked survivors stared straight ahead unblinking. Roy raised a clenched fist and thumb to the pilot. Parts of Mapinguari floated toward the rafts. A head bumped Juan's and Enrique's raft. A survivor glanced down and started trembling and went into convulsions. Others tried to back away and fell out. In the commotion Enrique wrapped the Mapinguari head in his jacket and hid it under the seat. A terrible stench mixed with black powder filled the air.

CHAPTER 6
PRESERVE

Two crew members dropped out of the gunship and waded into the river to help pull in the rafts. Roy and Mark were able to stay in the water because they had wetsuits on. They pulled to shore the people who had jumped out of their raft in a panic. A second chopper arrived. A crew member had blankets and several cold water survival suits. The co-pilot from the gun ship dropped four more survival suits. As survivors were carried ashore they were placed in suits or wrapped in blankets and carried to a helicopter. There wasn't space to load everybody. Roy, Mark, Juan, Horace, and a crew member from each helicopter would wait until a third helicopter arrived. "Give us all the assault rifles, grenades, flares and ammunition you can spare," Roy said. Helicopter crew members handed Roy and Mark several rifles and boxes. The six people on the ground started running to the farthest open space from the entrance to the river gorge and the Mapinguari robe on the tree as the helicopters lifted and flew down the meadow gaining altitude. The gun ship circled and strafed the woods before heading to Punta Alta with Henry, three dead and sixteen near dead.

When the pilot of the gun ship initially received the instructions to drop incendiary devices he sensed that extra support might be needed. He had requested another helicopter. The third helicopter was already leaving Punta Alta when the evacuation of the garden was taking place.

"Boss," Juan said, "we have company coming." A number of forms could be seen moving around at the edge of the woods. Five spears arced through the air and landed eighty feet in front of the armed group.

"Those throws could break the Olympic Javelin record," Roy said. "If they stay at the edge of the meadow we are okay."

"Maybe they consider the meadow out of bounds, out of their area," Horace suggested. "If that is the case, we are okay."

"Who says they know the rules?" Juan asked.

"I guess we didn't," Mark said. "We violated their space pretty good on the top."

"How in the hell were we supposed to know?" Horace asked. He paused, "My god, in the confusion I didn't see Peggy. Was she in the group?"

"Yes," Roy said. "I think she was in pretty rough shape. She should survive. Horace, I think her physical scars are going to be the least of your worries."

"What did they do to her?"

"Horace, I don't even want to imagine."

"Did they rape her?"

"Horace, anything you can think of probably happened, so stop thinking, don't ask, not now anyway."

Horace started screaming and running toward the woods firing his rifle.

Mark charged after and tackled him. A spear grazed Horace's outstretched arm. Mark dragged him by the pant legs out of spear range before taking his rifle from him and helping him to his feet.

"I'm sorry," Horace said. "I lost it. I just had to do something."

"Getting killed is not doing something."

"I know."

"Now we know they can do a lot better than the Olympic record," Juan said. "I wonder if they could pass the drug tests?"

The Andes and the plateau to the West blocked the afternoon sun. The shadows deepened and more Mapinguari could be seen gathering along the full width of the wooded boundary.

"Juan, put a flare up over the edge of the woods."

"Okay Boss." He pointed the flare gun at a high angle and pulled the trigger. The brilliant light accentuated the grotesqueness of the forms. Light reflected off their large eyes as they backed into the woods.

A shrill started sporadically in different parts of the woods then increased in intensity. As the light of the flare died out hundreds of the creatures emerged from the woods and lined up with spears raised. They started bobbing up and down.

Horace yelled and threw down his rifle and looked at his hands. "It burned me. It got so hot I couldn't hold it."

Juan dropped his rifle. "Mine too. How do they do that boss?"

"Some form of sonic induction. I guess they focus and if they have enough energy they can heat metal."

Mark asked, "What happens if they find the grenades?" He dropped his rifle.

"So far they haven't seen them," Roy said. "Juan, can you throw up another flare?"

The Mapinguari did not retreat. They started a slow synchronized walk forward forming a circle bobbing up and down.

The sound of helicopter blades beating the air filled the meadow. It hovered inches off the ground as everybody scrambled in.

"Don't shoot," Roy said. "Just climb as fast as you can out of spear throwing range." The helicopter surged upward with a steep banking motion, bottom side to the Mapinguari.

"Throw out all the food you have into the woods above them. Give them a reason to retreat then put a rocket into that pile of grenades. I don't want the Mapinguari to have them.

The pilot waited until the meadow was cleared and pulled down the targeting viewer over his right eye, clicked a couple of switches to arm a rocket, pressed a button on his control stick and banked to the right. A ball of light erupted in the field. Mapinguari disappeared into the woods.

"Mike, the pilot of the gun ship on the plateau said that when he dropped incendiaries, something caught fire the full length of the canyon. What's going on in there?" The pilot asked.

"We'll tell you when we know for sure," Roy said.

It was dusk when they approached the airport in Punta Alta. Miles away they could see red flashing dome lights on a dozen ambulances. Three blinking red beacons moved up the highway toward town. "Several people have already been taken to the hospital," the pilot said, "the others are ready to leave now. I am asked if you needed medical attention."

"Just bourbon. Lots of it," Roy answered.

The Commandante and Hector walked over to Roy and Horace as they jumped down from the helicopter. The downdraft blew cigar ashes on the Commandante's medal-festooned-blouse and he frantically swatted at them. "This is good," he said and "This is not so good."

He explained that several of the people who had come back had disappeared months ago. One was the son of a senator who had been taking a trail-bike tour south of Santiago. He was presumed dead, eaten by wild animals. Two others were lost hikers from Germany. The German Embassy had created lots of problems for the Commandante. Several of the captives were local natives from around the preserve who had strayed too close. Though word of their disappearance had filtered to the local police department, they were not a priority. "People have disappeared into the preserve for centuries. It is like quicksand. That is why we say, 'Do not go there!'"

Hector left and returned with clothes for Mark and Roy. Juan and Horace had dried out.

At the hospital Roy talked to the doctor in charge. "We have so little space and you have so many wounded. What has happened to them? They are like zombies, completely traumatized and so abused. It might be days before many of them can talk."

Roy looked at the doctor. "Mark and I will stay across the street for a week or so until we can talk with the survivors."

"Henry walked by and indicated he could stay a day or two." He wanted to find out more about the tools and customs of the Mapinguari.

Roy suggested he return to Seattle, "We will fill you in later. Now is not the time to do research."

"Understood." Henry walked down the hall. He asked a nurse where he could find some ice packs and left the floor.

Over a ten-day period Roy and Mark, and sometimes Horace, talked with the former captives. Horace knew all the GOE staff who had been lost in the three flights. Finding out how people had died and the torture and deprivations they endured deeply affected him. He saw

Peggy after she had been cleaned up and given a brief examination.

Mark had been outside the room when Horace went in. Horace literally stumbled out of the room, white and trembling. "That's not her. They have done something to her. She doesn't know me. I don't even think she saw me. Just blank eyes. Mark, what am I going to do? I don't think I can stand to see her again."

"Hang in there, Horace. She is in shock. It will take a few days. She will need your help"

"I can't do it." Horace left and didn't return to the hospital while Mark and Roy were there.

After ten days, five of the survivors felt they could leave the hospital. The doctor asked them to stay with friends nearby if possible and to come in each day for another week. Each admitted to having some bad dreams and moments of apprehension but otherwise felt they could return home.

It was two days after they were rescued before the tabloids got into high gear. The Commandante put the hospital off limits to reporters but not before some damage had been done. GOE had been good to the Commandante over the years and Mark made it clear that GOE did not want any reporters in the hospital.

Headlines read "Aliens Rape Hikers," "Pregnant Woman Rescued from Wilderness Beasts."

A week after the escape from the Preserve Mark was called into the Commandante's Office. "Your Mr. Horace has committed a murder. He shot the editor of the local newspaper that reported that a lady geologist was going to have an alien baby."

Mark quickly worked out an arrangement for Horace to be moved to Buenos Aires and put into a psychiatric hospital. The Commandante watched while Mark called Lars his boss in the Antarctic station, and lawyers in Belgium and Buenos Aires. "We work together. This is good," said the Commandante.

Roy and Mark agreed it was time to get back to Seattle and sort out the collection of stories and observations they had gathered. It was obvious the Mapinguari are resourceful and have capabilities that might never be understood.

On the plane Mark asked Roy what he thought should be done with the Mapinguari. "Leave them alone," Roy suggested. "Minimize the publicity and keep people away if possible. They have lived there for centuries apparently. It is their world. Science will have to wait until we know how to talk with them."

"Roy, how many of those little bourbons have you had?"

CHAPTER 7
SCINTILLATOR

"General Parker, Mark and I have seen a few things we don't believe. We believe the helicopter parts you spotted for us were deposited at the site by a group of Stone Age savages. They apparently used a network of ancient lava tubes, sort of an underground highway, to move the parts from the canyon thirty miles away. We didn't see the helicopters when we looked because they had already been dismantled and moved. Even if they had been in the canyon we would not have seen them because the sections of the canyon were cloaked by netting that was filled with gold, silver and other conducting materials. The canyon was effectively a giant screen room."

"You said they were Stone Age savages?"

"Sir, Mark and I had some very intense encounters with the occupants of the canyon. Also, we were able to extract twenty people who were being used as slaves. Ten of them were from the helicopters we were looking for. The others had been captured over a period of years. The people we rescued provided us with information about these savages and some of their capabilities."

"Sir, they are not human or at least not our species."

"Not human? Why do you say not our species?"

"The area has long been considered taboo and treated like a religious sanctuary. Apparently the entities that we started calling Mapinguari, have been taking captives for centuries. Besides using them for labor and food they have bred with them. The mortality rate is high but there are survivors."

"How could you possibly know that? What did you mean, food?"

"They eat dead captives. There were skulls with the helicopter parts you found. They had feasted on the brains and ate the remainder of the helicopter crew that could not be used as slaves. They are cannibalistic."

"The breeding?"

"Some of the people we got out had been there for several years. Perhaps they were so delusional, brain washed and filled with cultural lore that they didn't really know or see what they reported, but they indicated that they had seen newborns. They all described the constant coupling with female captives."

"Cross species mating isn't possible is it?"

"Tell that to a mule."

"I mean with humans."

"Mark identified a number of DNA similarities between the Mapinguari and humans, apparently enough that the breeding is possible. It seems, however, that some of the capabilities of Mapinguari are lost in the breeding and the survivors are removed from the colonies and wander the plateau and surrounding areas. The captives called them monks because of the Sotano they wore."

"The what?"

"Sotano, a cassock or burnoose, a hooded robe. Mark had seen hooded figures that the Chilean co-pilot called 'monks on a constant pilgrimage.' For centuries the locals have described what they have seen in terms of what they know. A hooded figure that wanders and does not speak is a monk. Where they walk is holy ground, spiritual ground. The preserve."

"Furthermore, the monks are in constant communication with the Mapinguari."

"You know of course," General Parker said, "that if I didn't know you and Mark, you two would be on your way to maximum security psychiatric ward. Might still have to if your story gets anymore far fetched."

"Send in the white coats," Roy said.

"Is there really any hard evidence that breeding is possible?"

"Well, there was a lady on the first helicopter. She is a geologist and was operating the DNAS. They apparently had coupled with her for nine or so days on a near-constant basis. After the fifth day they started sniffing her vaginal area after coupling. On the ninth day one of the creatures let out a high modulated squeal, as some of the captives described it, and marked her. After that it was the only one that coupled with her."

"Marked, how?"

"Covered her with its feces."

"The doctor who checked her out indicated she was pregnant. I told him that her fiancée had told me when we first started on the trip that they were going to have a baby. The doctor seemed to accept the story but indicated she had been badly mutilated in the vaginal area. Mark has had her transferred to a secure hospital in Colorado."

"Roy, I really don't think I like hearing this. It is disgusting and bizarre."

"Just animal behavior we gave up millennia ago."

"Are you suggesting that these are some form of evolutionary throwback?"

"I don't know what we have seen. I can't suggest what it all means."

"You said the non-lethal breeding resulted in loss of capabilities. What is an example?"

"There are apparently some regressive characteristics that result in outward physical deformities in the hands and face."

"One of the captives was a Swiss zoologist who had been presumed lost twenty years ago. He is in bad shape. He suggested that the creatures had two characteristics that he observed over the years that were lost. One was what we call ESP, extra-sensory perception, at least in terms of long distance communication, and a shared group mindset."

"And the other?"

"Sonic projection. They can emit and detect high frequency signals like a bat. Maybe it is an adaptation to living underground or an original DNA capability that allowed them to survive underground and avoid terrestrial predators."

"When we were surrounded by them and drew out weapons, they seemed to be able to focus their sound on an object. They were able to heat our guns to the point that we couldn't hold them. Like Archimedes destroying the Roman ships in the defense of Syracuse by using mirrors to focus the sun's rays on the sails of the ships and burning them."

"It takes the focused energy of three to drill a hole in a rock. In addition to smashing the helicopters with rocks, or slicing aluminum and steel with shards of flint sharper than a scalpel, a number of them working together could burn through metal."

"We did have the parts moved to McChord and analyzed them," Parker said. "The investigators wondered how parts were cut. They said some were just pulverized with rocks and flexed until they broke. Others had been sliced like in a metal cutting press but there were no microscopic metal remains of the blade. Other pieces had been burned through but there were no chemical traces of the torch used. Finally they found a number of pieces of metal that were completely crystallized and snapped off. This you are telling me was done with telepathic sonic beams?"

"As I said, Mark and I really don't know what exactly we have seen. The stories we have heard seem to fit the kind of physical evidence. Mark said that all of the parts of the helicopter were covered with urine and feces."

"That is what the lab boys said. They had to wear gas masks to work on the parts."

"You won't believe this but that was quality control. The creature that first got to a part to disassemble it peed on it to mark its possession. When the part arrived at the scrap yard on the plateau they defecated on it as a delivered check-off mark."

"Ugh," the General responded. "Now I know who assembled my new car. Roy, I have to go. What is emerging is a notion that these creatures can pose some kind of military threat."

"Three quick comments General before you go. They don't seem to see their capabilities as tools for global domination, only protection. Second, they have two DNAS units. Third, we think there are as many as sixty more captives in the other three canyons."

"What are you going to do, Roy? What if somebody else goes in there and finds them, their capabilities and these DNAS devices? Next time we talk be sure and tell me what DNAS units are and what you want to do about the canyons. Goodbye."

"Goodbye, Sir."

Mark entered the room when Roy finished debriefing the General. "Lunch?"

"Let's go to the cafeteria and punch up a panel scene of the Sahara desert where we can see everything that moves and is coming in our direction."

"So what did the General say?"

"He thinks he might want to lock us up in a mental ward. Before that, however, he thinks there might be an issue of national security and wants to know what I, we, are going to do about it."

"Let's eat first. When do you brief Max Schnell and Henry about what happened?

"Right after lunch. So far it should be easy. Henry doesn't know anything about DNAS. He only saw us after we came down the river and saw a bunch of savages throwing spears. Because of the rescue effort in the canyon we didn't have a chance to find the rocks we allegedly were originally looking for. The reason for Henry's being there wasn't found so there really isn't much we have to tell Max. It was an aborted mission."

"It will be nice if he buys your story. What's good on the menu?" Mark scanned the hologram over the table, showing what each options would look like. "You really have to add smell to the visuals." He tapped the table with the middle finger on this right hand like a blackjack player asking for more cards. With each tap the image of another plate of food appeared in front of him. He flicked the finger away from him and the previous meal reappeared. "That looks good. I think I'll have the Beef Stroganoff."

Roy rolled his eyes upward and sighed. "Here comes Conrad Blankenstaff. He works with Laney Smith. Remember Laney, the Head of GENXPLR, Genetic Exploration? Conrad often sits and kicks ideas around with me."

Conrad Blankenstaff was in his early thirties, short, slightly overweight and balding.

"Hi Conrad. This is Mark Stark. Mark, Conrad Blankenstaff. Want to sit with us?"

"You sure it's okay?"

"Sit."

"I understand you guys had quite an ordeal."

"How's that?"

"Enrique Salivare, at RENGCA, was on your trip, right? Well, he came back a week ago with the wild story about being chased by savages and all. Sounded horrific."

"We had our moments."

"That trip had something to do with DNA that I analyzed a couple weeks ago didn't it?"

"DNA?"

"Laney had given me some scrapings from an aluminum surface to analyze. It was bizarre stuff. He said I was just confirming a DNA study that had been done in South America."

"You are right. So much has happened I forgot about the sample Laney had." Roy smiled at Conrad hoping to sidetrack the discussion.

"Mark, you are the person who first analyzed the DNA. Is that right?" Conrad fingered the table display menu and made a selection without taking his gaze off Mark.

"What are you looking for, Conrad?" Roy asked. Roy looked from Conrad to Mark and back to Conrad.

"I am not sure exactly but what I have is the sense that you analyzed the DNA in the field."

"Yes," Mark responded.

"How?"

"I just scanned it, I mean scraped a sample. I had a small testing lab in the helicopter. Very special lab. Custom built for the company I work for. Very expensive."

"You said scanned. The rest was bull. How do you scan DNA?"

Roy broke in. "Conrad there are things we cannot discuss here."

"Okay."

A waitress delivered the meals. Mark had Beef Stroganoff; Roy had a large Crab Louie made with Dungeness crabs; Conrad had noodle soup.

"By the way, Roy, how did the Margolis case turn out? I understand the boy was acquitted."

"You are right and we greatly appreciated your help. We owe you one, Conrad."

"Can I see you this afternoon, after your debriefing with Max and Enrique?"

"I see my appointment calendar has been advertised to the public." Roy didn't try to hide his displeasure. "Yes, come on over, Conrad, by yourself."

Roy and Mark returned to Roy's before the meeting with RENGCA. "Roy, I slipped up didn't I? Sorry. He was like a weasel sniffing blood. Now what?"

"He is tenacious, isn't he? He is very bright and he does get excited at times over ideas. It probably doesn't do his heart much good. He has a heart murmur and a partially blocked valve but hasn't seen a doctor and doesn't know it."

"How do you know about his heart condition?"

"Remember the heart beat tracking system I mentioned? The staff of the tenant groups and most of the Wallace Images staff don't know about it. I've suggested to Conrad that he see a doctor, but he hasn't."

"Don't worry too much about his tripping you up. The Margolis case involved a kid working on a Top Secret project. Conrad is cleared. He probably would find out about DNAS from General Parker anyway. You can tell him what it is, and me for that matter, so I can tell the General what it is. He has staked National Security and diplomatic relations on it. Sooner or later he wants him to know what it is."

Roy entered Maximillian Schnell's office. Henry was there.

Maximillian bounded across the carpet with an outstretched hand and met Roy halfway across the room. "Good to see you. What a horrible, horrible trip you had. We didn't even get a sample of the rock you were looking for. Enrique here is distraught. Elmira has given him such a bad time about his screwing up, as she says, that he is thinking about quitting."

Roy explained the basics. They went into a wild area and found people who had to be rescued from fierce savages. The rescue precluded any search for the rocks that had been photographed from space.

"Henry was in no way responsible for what happened."

"Who were these savages?" Maximillian asked. "We certainly want to get them into our indigenous peoples data base in WIGS. We might have to go back. We want to type their DNA to support our cultural migration and diffusion studies. Enrique was not familiar with them and he is our South American expert.

Maximillian looked at Enrique. "I am hoping you will reconsider leaving and stay."

"Roy, I know you are busy and since there is nothing more to be said, let's go about our mutual schedules. Thank you for coming."

Enrigue stood and shook hands with Roy. "Thank you for the adventure. I am sorry you weren't successful."

Back in his office Roy beeped Mark.

"What's up?" Mark asked. "How did the meeting go?"

"It went fast. Conrad will be here in a few minutes. After this meeting I want you to get back to Punta Alta and find out who said what to Henry. He was on the first chopper that went out from the meadow."

"Understood. Here comes Conrad."

Roy explained to Conrad that the means of studying DNA that Mark had used had been classified and put into Pandora's Box.

"Conrad has worked with General Parker and knows the level of classification. You don't have to worry about what you say."

"Affirmative," Mark said.

Mark explained that the DNAS, which stood for DNA Scintillator, was a device developed to locate specific DNA patterns in rocks and shale and other potential oil bearing deposits. "We have samples of the DNA of the carbon based deposits that led to oil and coal fields. We have found that certain patterns have a high yield potential. We scan core samples with the DNAS for those patterns we know to have a high potential. We ignore sites with low DNA potential. The first model of DNAS required a direct scan. That is, the sample had to be in front of the scanner. The second model allowed greater distances and even small subsurface detection. The DNA could be detected through six feet of rock. We are trying to miniaturize a unit that we can drop down a hole. It would scan a column twelve feet wide. It will be a very efficient way to look for oil."

"Our third model, still at the prototype stage, can be used to study mineral replaced DNA. In terms of geologic processes, silicon and other minerals can replace the carbon molecules. Petrified wood and fish droppings are examples. The carbon in the DNA molecules is replaced. The pattern is preserved. The new model lets us scan fossils."

Roy and Conrad interrupted at the same time. "How does it work?"

"Atomic and molecular resonance. Think of a tuning fork at one end of a room and a piano at the other. Strike a key on the piano with the same frequency as the tuning fork. The tuning fork across the room will vibrate sympathetically with the sound waves. Dampen the piano keys and you can hear the excited tuning fork. Rather than a piano we have a DNA pattern code programmed into the DNAS. Rather than air as the carrier of energy we use a focused beam, a combination of a parallel rail, ringed plasma and neutrinos. The tuning fork is DNA. The DNA absorbs the energy at the atomic level and the molecular level. At the atomic level the atoms are energized driving the electrons to higher orbits. When the beam stops, the atoms return to their original temperature state which is a measure of their energy level. Some atoms, however, have forbidden states. A crazy term to describe energy wells that trap electrons at an elevated energy level. Once in the well an electron cannot drop to its normal level. Lasers and a lot of solid state electronics involved means of drawing energy from the potential wells. The ringed plasma excites the atomic structure and fills up the wells. The neutrino beam causes the energy to spill out. The energy release is detected as a scintillation on our display."

"There are lots of devices that involve molecular excitation. In the fifties a device called a Bohr-Magnetometer was used in mineral exploration. A magnetic field was placed around a bottle of deuterium. The magnetic field aligned the bipolar deuterium molecules and was released. The alignment required energy. When the magnetic field was released the energy was radiated. The rate of radiation was, or is, influenced by the earth's magnetic field. The radiated signal was used to detect mineral deposits that distorted the earth field structure."

"The same concept as the Bohr-Magnetometer is the basis of the Magnetic Resonance Imaging system,

MRI's, used by doctors to picture soft tissue in the body. Strong magnetic fields excite molecules in the body, which radiate energy. Initially MRI's were very large devices into which the patient was inserted. A couple of years ago the MRI concept was miniaturized for insertion into the body. Swallow the MRI which is attached to a string and pull it out when done."

"So you are telling us you can input a DNA pattern into your scintillator device and scan and detect that pattern at a distance, even through rock, and if the DNA pattern is in a million-year-old fossil you can detect it?"

"Yes."

"Jesus Christ," Conrad said, do you have any idea how potent a weapon this can be?"

"Why do think it has been put into Pandora's Box."

"Mark, you might or might not know that a lot of work I do involves old DNA patterns. I am interested in how you input your patterns. Right now we have lots of little bars on a piece of paper."

"It wasn't that big of a deal to develop a digitizing pattern for DNA. The digital process should speed up your pattern searches."

"Agreed. Holly, I think you have met her Roy, has been coming up with a system to digitally codify our DNA patterns. Do you have any shareware?"

"Even the concept of digitizing DNA is now top secret as far as you are concerned, Conrad. It is classified and you can't talk about it any further in your office."

"I'll lose my job."

"Remember, you opened the box and are now stuck with the consequences. Besides, that wasn't your department. It is Holly's."

"Now that you guys have screwed me with my own curiosity," Conrad said smiling, "May I see a sample of scintillated DNA?"

"Sure." Mark asked Roy if he could connect a WIGS terminal into Mark's computer in the Antarctic. Mark called Lars at the Ice House and indicated he was tapping into the computer system and not to worry, thinking a hacker had found a way through the security system.

"The following slides show an oil deposit we like and the DNA pattern we associate with it."

The first slide showed an ice field and a drilling platform. "This is one of our test holes in the Antarctic three years ago."

The next slide showed Mark with his hands cupped holding a mass of black goo. "Oil at minus ten Fahrenheit."

"This slide shows our digital printout and the conventional DNA pattern display."

"That looks familiar," said Conrad."

"Here are four slides taken at undisclosed sites showing the DNA found there. They represent samples with a poor potential for oil production. The sections of DNA that our analysts feel represent poor potential are marked."

"In the first the T-5 junction is too blunted. In this one," the slide appears on the monitor, "J-4 doesn't connect. In this last one," he says as he points to the middle of the row of vertical bars, "corresponds to the more popular version of the double helix pattern. This has a lot of artistic rendering and colors. In a couple of years we figure DNAS will be known and we want to have a nice chronological presentation of the concept. You can see in this pattern a missing carbon molecule."

Laughing, Roy said, "Oh yeah, I sure noticed that missing carbon."

Roy looked at Conrad. "What's the matter, Conrad. You look white as a sheet. The noodle soup get to you?"

"No, not that at all. Mark, can you go back to the second slide? It felt funny to me but I was so wrapped up in your presentation it didn't register."

Mark pulled up the second slide.

Conrad was shaking.

"Are you okay, Conrad? What can I get you?" Roy asked.

"Open my computer channel, code NOTLUCY. Access block TRI-98236. Put it on top of Mark's slide."

Roy punched a few keys and an image slid onto the monitor. He punched another combination and the two images superimposed.

For three minutes everybody seemed to hold their breaths. Roy and Mark turned and looked at Conrad.

Roy asked the only possible question. "They are the same. What is it?"

"That is what hominid DNA looks like regressed three hundred million years. That is man in the Triassic!"

CHAPTER 8
TRIASSIC

"Before you leave, Mark, where was that slide taken?" Roy asked keying in WIGS on his computer. An image of WIGS appeared. "This is not interactive but you can zoom in on the globe and show us. Use the mouse. We can save the coordinates and then run a WIGS session later."

"Let's see, Roy," Mark highlighted an area south and east of the preserve, "Here in the Pampas. GOE had limited exploration rights with a large cattle rancher. Fifteen holes. The owner probably sells exploration rights to every company that comes along."

"Roy, I had better go and follow up on Henry." Mark said, and then realized that he wasn't going to say anything about the trip to the Preserve. He looked at Roy and then Conrad, and back to Roy.

"No harm done," Roy said.

After Mark had left, Roy looked at the computer screen. "Conrad, if Mark's sample was here," pointing to the red spot on the monitor, "where would that have been in the Triassic, given plate drifting?"

"Let's go into WIGS and run a reverse simulation."

"You mean hop into your time machine."

As they walked to a WIGS room Conrad said, "I hope I am not out of place but was Mark trying to find out something about Enrigue. Does that have anything to do with his quitting?"

"What do you know about that?"

"Not too much. The scuttlebutt is he got back from your trip wired. You would have thought he had won the lottery. Apparently he brought back some rare find, at least according to Elmira. She was his roommate. He brought back something, and when she badgered him to see it to the point he got really pissed, he said it was a skull. He moved out that night."

"Roommates?"

"Weird relationship. She is a good looking woman. We've had coffee together a few times and I have run tests for her over the past year. She was too smart for him. I don't know what she saw in him if anything. They were both paranoid about what the other was doing. I guess they lived together to save psychic energy. It was easier to spy on each other. Go figure."

Roy and Conrad entered a WIGS observation room. There was an unscheduled time slot and since they were not running a classified model there was no problem starting. Conrad opened WIGS and selected a full sized model. He indicated to Roy that expanding the basketball sized globe floating in the middle of the WIGS space would take a few minutes.

"I will pull up a flat continental drift model. It will show the continents and tectonic plates without mountain relief or any minor rivers. The mid-Atlantic ridge and major ocean floor rift zones will be indicated. Areas of expansion on the ocean floors will be colored but fade out when expansion stops so we can see forces pushing the plates around."

Roy watched the small globe expand as the continents emerged from the light blue color of the oceans. They looked like the gray slate tile holograms on the floor in the main lobby.

Roy said, "It's amazing that when I was taking geology courses in the late 50's the concept of continental drift wasn't even established, and now we can simulate the evolution of the earth. A couple of my professors were disciples and advocates of Wegner's theory of continental drift proposed in 1912."

Conrad nodded, "He had a lot of good ideas but like anything else out of the mainstream, everybody is hell bent on rejection. I think it was Arthur Holmes in the thirties who figured it was thermal convection from a molten core that drove the process. His ideas weren't accepted until the 1960's."

A red light flashed to indicate the enlargement was complete.

"I'll key in the coordinates for Mark's drill site." He looked at the point Mark had made from Roy's Office. "FIX," he said. The point changed to a small red diamond in the twelve-foot-high representation of South America.

"Okay, Roy, here is what I am going to do. We will back up in time rather fast. If we let one second represent 500,000 years it will take ten minutes to back up 300 million years which takes us back to the regressed age of the DNA we are matching. We can speed it up or slow it down." Conrad keyed the size of each time increment and when to stop. "Go."

The continents on the globe started moving. "I told it to reverse time at 500,000 years per second and go back three hundred million years. If you wanted to see the sky darkening when volcano ash blots out the sun for a year you would not see it happen, too small a time interval. The data is in the system but it would really slow us down to ask WIGS to stop if it encounters such an event. Everything we think is known about the geology of the earth is accessible to WIGS. As the simulation goes back in time the Time Display will show the MYA or 'million years ago'."

The shape of the globe a few feet in front of the window started changing. The Himalayas flattened out and India started moving south. The islands in Micronesia disappeared. The Mediterranean opened toward the Indian Ocean. Europe and Asia started to pivot counter clockwise, hinged at the Straits of Gibraltar. When the time display indicated 14 MYA the Arabian Peninsula had closed onto Africa and both had drifted slightly toward South America, pulling away from Asia. The Mediterranean Sea opened to the east. Australia moved slightly south; Indonesia was subsiding. At 50 MYA Greenland and Europe moved back toward North America and a large body of water opened between Asia and the forerunner of the Balkan states. India separated from Asia. Australia moved toward Antarctica. With each passing second Roy visualized pages from past geology books.

Conrad pushed a pause button on the console. "Roy," he said, "you have to breathe."

"You are right. This is so spectacular. I was concentrating and forgot to breathe." Roy took a few deep breaths and straightened up. "Is there a way to get a feel for geological periods?"

"Sure," Conrad said. "This won't tax the system." He keyed in a request for a display of geological Periods. A data table appeared to the left of the globe, like a chalk board in a classroom and displayed the geologic Periods and upper age boundary for the Periods that had already passed. "Holocene (10,000 MYA), Pleistocene

(1.8 MYA), Pliocene (5.3 MYA), Miocene (23.8 MYA), Oligocene (33.7 MYA), Eocene (54.8 MYA)." Conrad said, "We are in the middle of the Eocene now. Anything else before we continue?"

Roy just shook his head and took a breath. Conrad hit the continue button.

Roy watched the silent movement of the continents and kept his eye on the red spot. Eocene moved up the board and "Paleocene (65 MYA)" appeared. India had moved halfway down to the Antarctic. South America had pulled away from Mexico and moved a little toward Africa. The mid-Atlantic ridge disappeared. Deep trenches flattened out. Roy was watching patterns, predicting in his mind how the continents would move. Questions would come and go. "Where is the Grand Canyon? When you raft through it you brush up against four-billion-year-old rock. It has to be here somewhere." Then he would remember to focus on the red diamond somewhere where South America used to be.

"Cretaceous (144 MYA)" slid up onto the board, the counter registered 150 MYA. Africa had moved west and was nearly touching South America, squeezing out the Atlantic Ocean. Asia was rotating north. India was descending to form a wedge between Africa and Antarctica. The Indian Ocean without India was transformed into a vast expanse of water known as the Tethys Ocean adjoining the Pacific.

Jurassic (206 MYA), Triassic (248 MYA), Permian (290 MYA), Carboniferous (354 MYA).

Roy had not been paying attention to time or even to the Period display table. He was mesmerized by the transformations.

At ten minutes South America, Africa, India, Australia and the Antarctic were connected as a single land mass in the Southern Hemisphere, to a single land mass that contained what is now Asia, North America and Europe. Pangea. Alfred Wegner had given the super continent the name Pangea, meaning "All-Earth."

At twelve minutes the parts that had come together to form Pangea were moving apart. Some of the land masses were the elemental continents. Others were large splinters of crustal plate pushed about by the convection currents of heating toward the core of the earth. The plates forming Florida and New England moved over to what appeared to be Africa. Roy blinked as if waking up.

Conrad said, "Earth to Roy."

Roy grunted.

Conrad indicated he had let the simulation run a couple of minutes longer than planned so Roy could see the formation of Pangea as well as its transition to today.

"What do we have?" Roy asked.

Conrad said he was going to fast forward fifty-five million years to the latter stages of the Pangea, in the Triassic Period.

"The drill site is in the middle of a band about three thousand miles wide that stretches across the southern part of Pangea, the super continent. That area rose and fell from dry land to low swamps with some inundation by warm seas. The guys over at RENGCA called this area DNA soup. Something similar was happening in the Northern Hemisphere. All kinds of life forms were developing and disappearing: Dinosaurs, rodents, placentals, mammals and cockroaches. There is some speculation that the earth was exposed to heavy radiation which played havoc with DNA, creating unimaginably large numbers of combinations and permutations of potential life forms. Some would take millions of years to emerge. There were life forms evolving and dying out naturally and through catastrophic extinctions that would only be seen later as fossils or fuels."

"So," Roy said, "if the DNA found was here," pointing to the diamond, "the source of the DNA could be part of the soup and spread across the band?"

"No reason to believe otherwise."

"Tag the band yellow and run the model forward in time."

The continents spread apart. North America, Europe and Asia moved north and spread to the east. Africa separated from South America, India raced up into Asia, the Himalayas grew and the eastern end of the Mediterranean closed kaleidoscopically.

Roy sat up straight and took a deep breath. "The world as we know it transformed in front of my eyes in ten minutes. This is unbelievable." He pointed to the tagged fragments of the former Triassic swamp area.

The yellow band ran diagonally to the southeast through Chile and Argentina, it ran across southern Africa and it covered the top half of India. The top of the Antarctic and the Western portion of Australia had some yellow.

"I wonder if we drilled in any of those places we would find a match to the DNA in Mark's slide?" Roy pondered.

"What might be more interesting," Conrad said, wheezing slightly and turning red, "would be finding DNA that matched a pattern with regressed DNA at ten million years."

"Are you okay, Conrad?"

"I'm fine Roy," Conrad said trying to downplay his excitement. "We find five-million-year-old sites here." He pointed to the Lake Baringo region of Kenya. The regions here and at Olduvai farther south have been dry and subjected to erosion. Bones are out in the open, just waiting for a keen-eyed local or researcher to find them. All these other places are either under mountain ranges, lush grasslands or ice."

"You are right," Roy commented. "There could be bones of people covered in landslides, volcanic dust, quicksand, or just plain buried all over places that can't be seen."

"Science is like English colonization," Conrad says. "The British hit the American shore and claim it all. An anthropologist finds a bone and lays claim to the origin of man and all future grant funding."

"What's the matter? GENXPLR doesn't have funding problems, does it? I thought RENGCA was the group fighting the limited establishment view, as Max calls it, when it comes to funding."

"As soon as WIGS suggests there are Genome patterns differentiating populations at fairly basic levels and we try to publish, all hell breaks loose. I, we, GENXPLR just don't get the credit we deserve."

"Look Conrad, relax." Roy said, "Even if we go out and drill and find suggestive DNA, it might not change anything."

"Understood. The established academic and scientific community doesn't like to be moved from its sacred cows. And don't forget the religious and political institutions. Even something as basic as plate tectonics took fifty years to be accepted."

"You have one thing working for you now that you didn't have before."

"What's that?"

"Knowledge that there is something there and a way to find it."

"You are right, Roy. Boy are you right."

"Isn't this bigger than GENXPLR?" Roy asked.

"I guess so." Conrad acted like he was giving up sacred turf. "Exploring this should include RENGCA and the WIGS staff."

"Don't forget GOE, Mark's group." Roy interjected. "They are the only one with access to DNAS. Also, there is the tight security issue. You are the only person at GENXPLR who can even know what we are involved in. Nobody at RENGCA has the clearance level. Only Jason Barnes is cleared at WIGS. Eugene Langley, Vice President for research for Wallace Images, is also cleared."

"Conrad, your specialty is genetics. Know anything about geology?"

"Not really, why?"

"Let's say we drill forty-five holes across in the yellow areas. I wonder what geologic features would increase our chances of finding something?" Roy asked.

"Can you just run around the world drilling holes?" Conrad looked at Roy.

"Exploration companies do it every day. The major problem is going to be how to do it without revealing our purpose. Got a good idea for a cover story?"

"One of our concerns in mapping genome patterns has been the effect of nuclear radiation on mutations. Maybe we could piggyback on the UN concerns over continued nuclear testing. We could say we are getting baseline data for the Southern Hemisphere."

"Might work. We have a few days before anything can be organized."

"Roy, what is that?" Conrad said looking at WIGS. "Somebody is interrupting our session."

WIGS transformed and an area north of Aconcagua to Punta Alta was expanded and shaded light orange. Light diagonal stripes covered the region of the canyons. South of Aconcagua and on the crest of the Andean mountain range a red circle enclosed Maipu, a 17,356 foot peak. A message appeared in a box at the top edge of the highlighted area. "POSSIBLE ERUPTION . . . 139 DAYS. . . SHADED IMPACT AREA (Ferdi)".

Roy picked up a phone and said "FERDI" and heard the target phone ring.

"Hi Roy. I guess you got my message."

Roy had asked Fernandez Canillas, a Wallace Images Fellowship recipient from the University of Barcelona, to map possible lava tubes above the canyons. Fernandez, who preferred to be called Ferdi by his friends, was a geologist and specialist in seismic tomography. Seismic tomography was a way of studying the earth's structure using seismic waves. Ferdi was locating data from different sources to load into WIGS. He had already asked Roy if GOE could set off some seismic charges on the plateau.

"Ferdi, I haven't had a chance to ask Mark for your blasts. What is going on?"

"Roy, there were some small quakes that gave me the data I needed. I have some mapping of the lava tubes. I could use more data but what we have already shows connections between the tubes in the different layers. Looks like a huge subway system."

"You might have a problem though. As indicated on WIGS there is probable eruption that might cover some parts of your canyon area. It doesn't look like it will be very big. I wouldn't send anybody there unless you have a really big reason to be there. Some of the gases that come from the type of eruption we expect are deadly."

"Thanks for the tip, Ferdi. I'll catch up with you later about what you have found so far. Bye."

"Is Ferdi anticipating that a volcano is going to erupt where you guys were?"

"Big time problems. Remember, we are in Pandora's Box."

"Understood," Conrad replied.

"We found an indigenous tribe living in the canyons. They apparently use a network of connected lava tubes to move to the surface and between canyons."

"Sounds like ants."

"Mark has lost two DNAS units to them and they apparently have sixty or so more captives in the canyons."

"Are you going to try to get them out before the eruption?"

"Ferdi was positive it would happen. I am not sure the occupants would want to leave. Also, I wouldn't know where to relocate them."

"Fort Dix and other military bases are sometimes used to house refugees until they can resettle."

"I don't think Fort Dix is ready for this group. Let me get together with you in a couple of days about where we might put those forty-five holes. Oh, before I forget. Thanks for running the simulations for me."

It was late and Roy drove home in a stupor. On each turn on the road he visualized a continent breaking away from Pangea and starting a slow drift to its current position on the globe.

"What do you mean, married?" Roy said looking from the maps spread on the table. "Juan, you just got divorced."

"Boss, every time I go on a trip with you I nearly get killed. When I get back I am so glad to be alive I have to share it with somebody. How can you share the joy of life without being in love, to make love?"

"Why don't you just stay married so there is somebody to come back to."

"They never understand me. They get too possessive. They don't understand that my working for you might take me away for long periods. They start nagging me to get a steady job at home. Do you know how boring that might be?"

"Possibly." Roy laughed. "In the mean time you will probably have three weeks to get divorced."

"Where are we going?"

"You don't want to know."

The phone rang. Juan picked it up. "Juan here. Roy Graham. Yeah. I'll call him. For you boss. It's the police."

CHAPTER 9
HENRY

"Elmira was found dead," Roy said. "Groundskeepers at the University of Washington Arboretum found her body in a dense grove of ornamental bamboo near the Pagoda. Apparently my name was on a piece of paper in her pocket, along with something that looks like a large bat ear. The officer on the phone said that normally I might be a suspect but his commanding officer, Leland MacFarland, vouched for me. You've met Mac – three doors down the hill, gray house."

"Right," Juan said.

"Mac asked if I could go down to the crime scene."

"You said Mark was going to call from McGurdo Bay. What should I tell him?"

The phone rang. "Hold on," Juan said. "That might be him now."

"Mark, good to hear from you. Your timing couldn't be better. What have you heard about Henry?"

"Sure I remember Walt," Roy said. "Walt Woldonski, he gave us the high sign to move into the garden. Tough guy. It's nice to know he is doing okay."

Roy listened to Mark and summarized for clarification and to keep Juan abreast of the conversation.

"So Henry talked to Walt and a few others who were capable of talking and got the idea that there was a lot of gold and silver stashed in the caves. Is there any suggestion that Henry has any hint that the Mapinguari are anything other than spear throwing locals?"

"Walt thinks Henry might have grabbed a head from the river. From an anthropological view, he struck gold in more ways than one."

"Mark, something just came up here. Henry's roommate was just found murdered. I am on my way to the crime scene now. Is there a chance he might show up down there and try to go back to the canyons?"

"BelGeo. Who are they?" Roy listened to Mark.

"Let me get this straight," said Roy. "A mining conglomerate from Belgium has told the Commandante they are to fly out of Punta Alta to the West. He advised them to stay away from the Preserve. A lot of good that will do if they think there is gold there. You say the Commandante thought he saw Henry in one of the BelGeo helicopters. Give the guy a big box of his favorite cigars."

"I think we had better have General Parker explore isolating the Preserve. With two DNAS units still there we have a concern. Also, if BelGeo ticks the Mapinguari off they might kill the other sixty or so captives."

"Thanks, Mark."

"Juan, would you see if you can find out when Henry left town? Check the airlines. He might have gone back to Punta Alta or to Belgium then to Punta Alta. Also, contact General Parker's Office. Let Maggie know I will call at 14:30 his time."

It was a short ride past the Volunteer Park Art Museum to East Galer down the hill off Capital Hill to the winding road through the Arboretum. The Pagoda was a gift from Japan to Seattle after an earthquake in 1923, thanking those that had provided support.

"Hi, Mac. What happened?"

"Looks like she was hit with a blunt object and placed here after the fact. Detectives have been to her apartment. They indicate there are signs of a struggle. Some type of tall ebony statue, big boobs and butt, was found on the floor with blood on it. There was blood smeared on the floor. The pattern had a straight edge, like the victim fell on a rug and some blood spread to the wood floor. There was no trace of the rug there or here. We haven't had time to confirm if the statue was the murder weapon but it looks like it."

"How about her roommate, Enrique Salivare, where is he?"

"We haven't located him. His belongings had been removed. Looks like he skipped. What do you know about him?"

"He was on a trip with us a short time ago. Henry works, or worked, at RENGCA a group at Wallace Images. You have been there. He apparently quit a day or two ago. There is a possibility he went to Belgium and then to South America. I talked to an associate before I came down here. He thought that Henry was in Punta Alta this morning."

"We will check the airport for his car. If he did this, what was his motive?"

"Mac, that's your job. I have some ideas but you work your side and we can compare notes later."

"Fair enough. Oh yeah, before I forget. This is the thing she had in her pocket with the note." Leland MacFarland pulled a plastic evidence bag from his pocket. Inside was the ear from a Mapinguari. "Somebody said it was an ear of some type. What do you make of it?"

"Mac, it is an ear from something we saw in South America. It is exceedingly rare. I have an idea that Elmira was trying to get it to me as evidence about something Enrique Salivare is planning to do. Mac, I know that your lab people will learn nothing from this ear. In fact, it will create so many problems you will wish you hadn't found it. I can use it and need it for several reasons that cannot be discussed. I think you know what I mean. If you can give it to me or have me sign for it we will both sleep better. It will be secured if you have to have it. I know you will be putting yourself out on a limb on this."

"Hey, Gillispie," Mac shouted to the plain clothes detective kneeling near the body. "Where is that thing, that ear, you guys found?"

"I think one of the lab crew got it."

"Gee, Roy, I think we lost that ear I wanted you to look at."

Roy drove to Wallace Images. When he got to his office he called Conrad's extension. "Conrad, can you run a DNA test on something for me? Okay, I'll bring it over to your office."

Laney Smith was in Conrad's office when Roy arrived. "Hello Roy, what brings you to the inner sanctum of GENXPLR?"

"I was hoping Conrad might do a DNA analysis on some tissue Juan found on our last trip. It's part of his bug collection."

"That ill fated trip. Wasn't Enrique on that trip? It is a shame he quit, Maximillian thought a lot of him."

"Quit? How do you know that?"

"I had lunch day before yesterday with Maximillian. He said Enrique had quit. Didn't give a reason."

"It was good to see you again, Roy. I have to run. Oh, Conrad, I have to cancel our afternoon meeting." Laney left.

"Okay, Roy, what do you have?"

Roy handed the evidence bag to Conrad. Static electricity had made the second bag containing the note stick to it. The second bag fell on the floor. Roy's name had been written on the back of a restaurant receipt. Conrad picked the second bag up and handed it to Roy. " Canles, good restaurant. I think it is one of Laney's favorite places to eat."

"What the hell is this thing?" Conrad extracted the ear with forceps and snipped a piece of tissue from the inside of the lacerated section.

"I think it is an ear off the skull Henry pirated from our trip."

Conrad replaced the ear into the bag and it gave back to Roy. He put the small piece of tissue into a mortar, added some liquid and ground the materials until the tissue dissolved. The contents were placed on top of a ceramic filter in a test tube and placed in a centrifuge. "We put the liquid that is strained through the microscopic pores in the filter into the GENXPLR DNA extractor, an automated DNA analyzer. It will take ten minutes. We might as well get a cup of coffee, lab style."

A beaker filled with coffee sat on a hot plate. Conrad opened a cabinet and took down two small chemistry flasks and poured coffee into each. "Another hour and that stuff will be black goo on the bottom of the beaker. "Let's go into the other room where there is a window."

In the distance, a tugboat towing a barge piled high with semi-truck-sized containers was heading toward the Straits of Juan De Fuca then Alaska. Two fishing boats were heading south to go around Magnolia Bluff toward the Ballard Locks, which separates the salt water of Puget Sound from the fresh water of Lake Union and Lake Washington. The Victoria Princess, a large ferryboat, was northbound to Vancouver, British Columbia. The snowcapped Olympic Mountains were silhouetted against a blue cloudless sky.

"A truly marvelous view." Roy said. "By the way, how much do GENXPLR and RENGCA work together?"

"Not very much. I've had the feeling that Laney frowns on GENXPLR staff getting together unless it is a project he is working on. Seems a little narrow-minded given the potential overlap of interests. On WIGS it seems that RENGCA cultural migration studies are almost the same as our Genome migration efforts.

RENGCA's stuff seems more statistical and iffy. We can only work with real samples."

"Do Laney and Maximillian get together often?"

"No. Their having lunch together surprises me."

"Now why doesn't this surprise me?" Conrad said looking at the computer display of the DNA analysis. "Look at this." He pressed a few keys on the computer console and another pattern appeared. He superimposed the two. "It is the same pattern as the sample I did for you before your trip. The scrapings from the helicopter parts. Was whoever owned this ear one of the spear throwers?"

"Yes," Roy answered.

"Those guys aren't human? Who are they? Where did they come from?"

"Conrad, if you started with your pre-hominid DNA and worked forward, what kind of perturbations would it take to get to this pattern?"

"What are you suggesting? That the pre-hominid DNA evolved into this rather than humans?"

"I never thought evolution was a linear process. A cosmic ray here, a cosmic ray there, a few non-lethal mutations and there is another branch on the evolutionary tree. This branch went underground."

A red light flashed over the door to the hallway. "Emergency phone call. Let me get it. Usually we don't like phones ringing in here so we use flashing lights. Conrad here. You want Roy? He is here."

"Roy. Hi Mark. Wow. I will get back to you in a couple of hours."

"Conrad, I have to go. Mark indicates that a BelGeo helicopter has disappeared in the Preserve."

"Who are they?"

"Conrad, it is imperative that none of this is mentioned to anyone including Laney. BelGeo is an exploration company we think Henry has teamed up with to return to the Preserve. There is a chance that Henry is in one of the canyons."

CHAPTER 10
WATCH

"Hello, General Parker."

"Roy, you have called me more in the past month than in the last five years. You must be having lots of fun. What do you need?"

"Two of your Pandora's Box devices were lost in the canyon we extracted GOE's crew and others from. One of the anthropologists at RENGCA, who had been with us, has skipped and teamed up with a Belgium company to go back to the canyon. In addition there are 40 to 60 people still in the canyons. What I suggest is a continuous satellite monitoring of the area and a military quarantine. If you see anyone going in, intercept them."

"You are stretching us Roy. I'll do whatever I can. I almost hate to ask, but is there anything else?"

"And now that you mention it, for more academic purposes, we want to do some core drilling in South America, Africa, India, Australia and Antarctica. Probably forty or so holes total. We need a cover."

"And you are suggesting?"

"We were thinking of getting baseline radiation measurements to support the analysis of future nuclear testing or the banning of such, whichever sticks best. We don't want the drilling to appear as a GOE operation. Remember the Mohole project. Basically it was a science project, using Howard Hughes' ships that had a spin-off in supplying naval intelligence data."

"I don't know, the nuclear testing stuff is wearing thin. Any other approaches?"

"How about a site survey for the locations of several deep space satellite stations? A joint research project with several NATO countries."

"We can make that work. When do you want to start and where?"

"I want to see if WIGS can suggest the candidate sites. It will be a couple of days."

"Roy, before you sign off, the lady you brought back from the canyon. She is still in bad shape. The doctors are saying the shock she has suffered is heavy-duty stuff. They feel she has no idea who she is or what has happened to her or when she will recover. Also, she is pregnant but all the blood chemistry and sonogram data is puzzling them. They know that this is some secured operation and want direction."

"General, nobody is ready for a cross-species birth and she is not competent to participate in a decision. Abort immediately and have the embryo destroyed in an acid bath so no DNA remains. I want sign-off by three people that witness its destruction. The medical staff does not have to know the particulars of the pregnancy."

"What about the science opportunity?"

"We know where the sperm came from. There is no reason why in vitro fertilization couldn't be used, basic data gathered and the product destroyed. There is no reason to use people as experimental receptacles."

"Understood. Surveillance has already started on the plateau. I'll let you know if anything shows up. We are going to try some new x-ray devices to penetrate the nets you described."

"Good-bye, General, thanks for your help."

"Eugene Langley, come into my office, I haven't seen you in months," Roy gestured to a chair in front of his WIGS monitor.

Eugene Langley had worked undercover at Wallace Images, before the ill-fated management retreat in Alaska, to find a source of industrial espionage. He had been with the CIA and retired after returning from Alaska. The President and the Director of Research of Wallace Images had been killed on the trip. The President's younger brother took over the company and Eugene assumed responsibility for Research and Development.

"Let me bring you up to date on a number of developments. I am hoping Wallace Images can be the organizational vehicle for drilling some core samples at sites around the southern part of the globe. Where is to be determined."

Roy described the DNAS developed by GOE, its potential and that it had been put into Pandora's Box. Eugene had met General Parker after the earthquake in Alaska at the end of the two-week management retreat. Eugene and Wallace Images were doing some work for General Parker. Roy knew that a relationship existed but did not have a need to know so had not inquired.

"Your projects are always interesting. How could I possibly say no? What do you want?"

Roy explained to Eugene the relationship that Conrad and Mark had found between oil bearing Triassic deposits and regressed hominid DNA. Further exploration of where the core sample materials had been deposited raised questions about other locations of pre-hominid DNA sites and evolutionary patterns.

"Can we run WIGS from a geological perspective to find candidate sites for drilling? Given all the forces of erosion, tectonic plate movement, volcanism, glaciation and so forth, WIGS should be useful in mapping areas of high potential."

Eugene nodded, "Why don't you and Juan meet with Jason Barnes in the morning? I'll let him know what you are interested in. We will identify a couple of sites and run some trials. If that looks promising we will go for a few more. Be prepared to spend a few minutes. Jason thinks of WIGS as a time machine and will take you back to the beginning of time."

CHAPTER 11
SURFING THE TETHY'S SEA

"Three hundred million years ago Pangea formed from the existing land masses, Gondwana and northern continents. Shallow seas rose and fell over the next 150 million years. The Southern Hemisphere was awash with tides of life forms. When we look at the composition of fossil records," Jason said to Roy, "it looks like a DNA soup existed for 100 million years. All kinds of critters were evolving, and dying out."

"Can I have dinosaur noodle?" Juan smiled at his own joke.

"Sorry, Juan, that won't be on the shelf for another 45 million years."

"The huge land masses collided forming Pangea and then started to break apart. Like bumper cars at the fair, the collision is an instant in geologic time. The bumper cars spin a little, get a new direction and continue on. The continents are a little more fragile. The pieces that came together fragmented and slowly came apart as they moved on."

"What is powering the movement of the land masses?"

"Heat. The top 400 miles of the earth, the mantle is molten except for the very top. The crust, the part we walk on, varies in depth from 2 miles, at the thinnest spot somewhere at the bottom of the Pacific, and 75 miles under the higher mountain ranges. The crust and the top 40 miles of the mantle are made up of plates that are moved around by the thermal gyres under them."

"The 400-mile-deep mantle probably looks like a lava lamp in very slow motion, with blobs of hot material rising and blobs of cooler material sinking or being pushed down as part of the subduction process when a plate is pushed under another." He ran his fingers over the control panel that looked more like an organ keyboard than a computer.

The outer layers of the WIGS dissolved into a transparent ghost. Jason pushed on some knobs, pressed on others and hit a few keys. The sphere slowly expanded from six feet in diameter to twelve. A reddish glow begins to form in the depths of the sphere. WIGS was peeling away the top 40 miles of the earth's surface.

Let's expand to the maximum. The earth will be 30 feet high and closer to 35 feet wide at the Center. We'll peel away the outer 40 miles." The expansion was gradual.

Juan remarked, "Looks like someone blowing up a large balloon."

"Even at this size we can get only a sense of what the top of the mantle looks like at a given point in time. There are some good hints where volcanic activity is likely even at this resolution. Those bright areas the size of a pea are hot spots."

"Let me show you the area near the Easter Islands west of South America."

"Jason," interrupts Malcom, a geophysicist working with Jason, "how about the Wellington hypothesis?"

"Okay, I gave you guys the simplistic explanation. There was a debate a few years ago about the thermal activity of the mantle. The original thought was that the mantle was one layer with thermal activity going from bottom to top. As Seismic Tomography developed, some people believed that the mantle was actually stratified and there was no exchange of materials between layers."

Malcom explained, "At a party last year John Wellington was staring at his unshaken martini and had a cerebral flash. He called Jason and me over and said, 'Watch.'"

"He dropped an olive into his drink. He simply said 'Eureka!' and smiled."

Jason said, "You've had one too many, John. Newton already said that when he realized olives are pulled by gravity into martini glasses."

"And," I said, "Archimedes observed that the olive displaces the contents of the glass."

Malcolm continued, "'No, no,' Wellington was saying as he gulped down the martini, spitting out the olive. 'Mike, give me another martini just like the last one, poured gently, no stirring.'"

"He held his fresh martini up so we could see. At the boundary of the gin and vermouth there were little swirls of fluid catching the blue and white flashes from the klieg lamp. He asked us, 'What do you see?'"

Jason said two liquids, stratified into two layers in a crystalline container reflecting lights.

Wellington had continued his demonstration, "Now watch," he said as he stuck an olive on a green toothpick slowly into the drink.

"What did you see?"

Jason answered, "Itsh, obvious. Your last drink put you over the edge."

Malcolm repeated his observation, "When the olive went through the boundary between the vermouth and gin, a perturbation occurred and there was mixing of the fluids around the olive. Minor eddies developed around the olive that broke away and swirled around in your glass. If you were sober and could have held your glass still the currents might have died out."

"Absolutely," Wellington had postured as he pulled out the toothpick and olive and swallowed the martini. "Let's get back to the lab."

"What?" Jason had said.

"I may be drunk but my brain can still drive."

Malcolm continued to describe what happened when they got back to the lab.

"Let's assume the mantle is stratified like your friend Jason thinks," he said to Malcolm, again smiling. "What if there is a major disruption that perturbates the boundary?"

Jason snorted, "Like God dropping a really big olive into his favorite drink."

"Or, I'd say, a large meteorite, or even a big earth-quake," Wellington had finished.

"Yes, yes, yes. Let's go get WIGS."

"Punch up meteor strikes," Wellington had instructed, "There are a couple of big ones back in the Triassic about 214 million years ago. Okay, crank WIGS back to 214 MYA and highlight the meteorite coordinates."

A display shimmered in the air in front of the control console.

John read out the display quietly to himself: Rochechouart in France, fifteen miles in diameter; Micouagan in Canada, sixty miles in diameter. There is another in Manitoba.

"Jesus Christ, look at that. They line up."

"What is WIGS doing now?"

"It just did a data search on other meteor strike research and found the same thing we just did. John G. Spray, at the University of New Brunswick, reported the linearity a couple of years ago. Must be a smart guy. First time I've heard of someone correlating a meteorological event with the structure of the earth at the time of the event without WIGS."

"So John came up with the idea of cataclysmic perturbations in the mantle. How does that tie into plate movement?" Roy asked.

WIGS had reached the maximum size.

Jason said to Roy, "Lets isolate a three-dimension view of the Pacific."

Juan observed, "Looks like a marble with red, blue, and green bubbles inside."

"It does, doesn't it. The red bubbles are hot magma, the stuff that comes out of volcanoes. The blue bubbles and slabs are the subducting cooled-off crustal materials. They will heat up, melt down and mix with the rest of the mantle matrix, the green colored areas."

Roy asked, "Can we get a sense of how this stuff moves in time?"

Jason pressed the "Simulate" key on the console. An array of icons of possible variables appeared on a clear panel in front of him. As he pressed several of the buttons the icons lit up. He pressed the "time icon," typed *15K* on a keyboard. Another icon window appeared and he typed *5M* and pressed "Initiate." The globe faded.

Across the space of the room that had held the holographic image of the earth Roy could see several people in other glass-enclosed booths looking back.

"Who are they?" Juan asked.

"I don't know," Jason answered, "this is an unsecured demonstration we are running. There are several other projects going on. We might be interrupting their activity. My login code usually bumps others out. They might be waiting for us to finish or they might be documenting what we are doing.

"Unless it is a secured use any number of authorized people can watch."

A buzzer sounded three times. Jason indicated the simulation was initialized and pushed the "Start" button. The globe materialized. The pattern of red, blue and green blobs in the mantle matrix was different than that which they had been looking at.

"That is the matrix thermal distribution our data base has for the period fifteen thousand years ago We are going to simulate the pattern from then until now. Fifteen thousand years in the next five minutes."

"To give you some idea of what is happening I've projected a vertical line down the center. You can see how far the different land masses are from each other."

A large red mass welled up along the West Coast of North America, Canada and Alaska. A smaller one appeared west of Mexico and Central America. Another appeared west of South America.

Juan pointed, "What is that hot spot doing in Antarctica?"

Roy said, "Mt. Erebus."

Jason pointed to other hot spots east of Japan in Indonesia and in the middle of the Pacific Ocean extending from Hawaii south. "The Ring of Fire," He said. "Notice the blue areas forming at the top and moving east and down. The cooling areas get heavy and slide under the lighter warm area."

"These can't be generated from actual data. There would be too many data points."

"Right, WIGS uses fractal creations bounded by some real data and algorithms on how we think liquids, in this case, behave. Every time somebody has a new idea we crank in the implied equations and rerun a simulation to see if WIGS fits better with that observation."

Distorted red masses moved upward and blue masses formed and moved downward.

A two-dimensional vertical cross section running from Japan to the tip of South America was displayed to the left of the sphere. The observation of gyres of magma rising and spreading and cooling under the base of the continental plates was dramatic.

"If you want music we can play the Rites of Spring synchronized with the eruption of volcanoes on the West Coast. You won't see the eruption, only a slightly changed aerial view. Looks like bubbles popping in a pot of boiling mush."

Jason said, "There goes Mt. Mazama in Oregon, Mt. Adams, Mt. Rainier." Mt. St. Helens and Penitubo in the Philippines changed shape as the simulation clock flashed "0" and the image froze.

Jason looked at Juan, then Roy. "Roy, there is something I want to show you. It will be secured which means no one else can see, monitor, or record what happens."

Roy looked at Juan and gestured with his chin toward the door. Juan said, "I'm going out to get some coffee." He left the room along with Malcom.

"I am sorry that Juan had to leave but the issues go beyond me. I want to run a scenario on WIGS without a lot of explanation. With everything else you have seen I will be interested in your interpretation."

Jason reset WIGS for another simulation. "300 MYA Gondwana and northern continents were colliding creating Pangea." He set the starting point for 230 MYA. "Two hundred and thirty million years ago the land masses had moved together. We think meteor impact perturbed the lower mantle layers enough that normal land mass drift was accelerated. There might even have been the formation of forces to create new plates. But new plates are not what I want to focus on."

One-hundred fifty MYA three large land masses Eurasia-North America, Africa-South America and Antarctica-Australia-India had formed.

"At the beginning of the simulation I will paint a red band across the middle one-third of the lower hemisphere. It crosses over what will become the southern half of South America, the top two-thirds of Africa, India, Australia and the top of Antarctica. What I am interested in is India."

"Why India?"

"The Indian plate starts off below Africa and has an unprecedented rate of advancement northward. About 65 million years ago another meteor impact created the 113-mile-wide Chicxulub crater in the area of Yucatan Peninsula and stimulated the mantle again. That was the impact that is credited with wiping out the dinosaurs. The African Plate was already moving toward Europe and India had split off from the Antarctic-Australian plate and was heading north. The perturbation might have caused magma upwelling at the southern end of India between the larger African and Antarctic plates. Think of the upwelling as a wave that was forced northward."

"Let me guess," Roy said, "India surfs the magma wave."

"Right. The Tethy Ocean was the name given to the body of water north of the Antarctic. It eventually becomes the Indian Ocean and to some extent the Mediterranean. India surfs the Tethy for 120 million years until it slams into Asia."

"Forms the Himalayas where it hits."

"Right again, and pushes the land mass to 29,000 feet. Of course the rising of the land is gradual and any life forms at the northern leading edge of India had a chance to adapt to the eventual rise in altitude and changes in the weather. As the Himalayas pushed the Asian plateau higher, dramatic weather evolved and weather and life on earth changed."

"Over the course of three hours and two hundred and thirty million years of simulation, all the continents moved into their current locations. After India crashed into Asia, polar caps formed and great sheets of ice advanced and retreated several times."

Roy was mesmerized by the dynamic view in front of him. Every now and then he realized he was holding his breath and had to remind himself to breathe.

The simulation clock had registered "230,000" for a number of minutes before he sensed Jason was in the viewing booth with him.

Jason said, "I think I know what you are feeling. Not necessarily a religious statement but it is like watching God create the world we know. Floods and all."

Roy took deep breath. "That is an unbelievable experience."

"What do you see?"

"More than olives in a martini. Actually a martini would be great."

"What do you see?"

"Wait, the simulation hasn't finished. We still have 230,000 years to go. Why?"

"Notice the red shading? The remnants of the red band we drew at the beginning?"

"What does red shading mean?"

"I am not going to say yet. I want you to notice where it is now."

Roy looked at the huge globe in front of him. A band of red shading went across the southern two-thirds of Africa. A band of red extended in both directions across the top of India where it intersected Asia, a band of red cut across the bottom third of South America. Small pockets of red shading appeared in Western Australia and northwest Antarctica.

"Okay, now what?"

"We will finish the simulation." Jason pushed "Continue."

The simulation clock digitally scrolled down to "0" and the screen froze.

Roy looked at the globe and still had to force a breath. In the last two minutes of the simulation the Himalayas had pushed up, there were flashes of white patches pushing down over Canada and retreating, islands appeared, disappeared and reappeared in the Micronesian archipelago area. The red shading had expanded up the East Coast of Africa and to the West. The red band over India moved west and north over China and into North America and down the West Coast. It also expanded west and spread into Europe and dropped down into northern Africa. The red shading in South America moved up the West Coast and diffused eastward. The shading in Antarctica spread and disappeared. The shading in Australia diffused slightly along the West Coast and into small island areas to the north.

"Time is up. Another team needs to use WIGS."

Roy looked at Jason. "I have an idea what you are driving at. It will take a little while to process."

CHAPTER 12
DRILLING SITES

"What can WIGS tell us about drilling sites?" Roy asked.

"Conventional wisdom suggests for man to evolve and survive required a savanna structure and someplace to hide like caves and trees to get away from some predators. There are detractors from the scenario but who really knows?"

"Within the fragments of the Triassic belt, which areas had that kind of terrain in the time frame eight to fifteen million years ago?"

"I can input our data request offline," Jason said, "and as soon as we can get back on WIGS we can ask the questions. WIGS will be free in three hours. Do you want to go get some dinner while we wait?"

"No thanks, Jason. I need to take a jog along the beach. I'll see you at 23:00 hours."

Roy started down a trail that cut across the clay and sandbanks of the bluff and his beeper sounded. If it isn't somebody I know, he thought, I'll call back tomorrow. It was General Parker. Roy jogged up the path and into his office.

"General, you beeped."

"A short message. Another helicopter has shown up at the old scrap site along with your DNAS units. At least that is what I think they might be. Your netmail has photos."

Roy punched in the codes for his netmail and printed the photos.

"When can you have the items picked up?"

"Choppers are on their way for salvage and a gun ship is sitting back a few miles keeping a watch."

"General, do not allow them to sit on the ground in the boundary of the Preserve. There is a nomadic group that we think is linked to the Mapinguari. They eluded instrument detection the last time Mark was up there."

"Hold it, Roy, I have a priority call."

"Roy, I am back. We have confirmation of your concerns. A gunner left the bird to take a leak. A spear sliced through his flack jacket like cheesecloth. Spears punctured bulletproof housings and cut fuel lines and some hydraulics. They managed to move back ten miles before all systems quit. Reinforcements have been dispatched. You said these were stone-age creatures. What the hell is going on?"

"Be sure you operate in the day time and avoid anybody and anything that moves. Watch out for religious looking types in robes. They are the ones that got your bird."

"One last footnote for the day. Mark indicates that BelGeo, a Belgium mining company just lost a chopper in the canyon. Probably the one you found at the scrap site. Enrique Salivare, the anthropologist who was on our trip was being taken to the Preserve area by BelGeo. He is also wanted for murder in Seattle."

"You are full of surprises, Roy," The General said. "Talk to you in the morning."

Roy went back to the bluff, climbed down to the beach. He jogged for an hour to the West Point Light. He watched the navigation beacon at the tip of Magnolia Bluff and the northern edge of Elliot Bay sweep its light across the dark horizon. A cool mist drifted off the water. Roy stretched and returned to Wallace Images.

"Are we ready, Jason?" Roy asked over the intercom.

"Meet you in the WIGS room in five minutes."

Roy drank a cup of coffee and went to see WIGS.

"Hi Roy. I got here a couple of minutes ago and initialized our run. The height and color of the wire framed peaks represent probability of find. The high red peaks are where you should drill."

"Send Mark a copy of the photos for South America, Africa and India. We can come back at a later date and look at the other sites."

"What looks good to you, Jason?"

A warning light blinked, WIGS blanked out. Eugene Langley entered.

"Aren't you guys up past your bedtime?"

"What about you?" Jason asked as he redisplayed WIGS.

"Why should you two have all the fun? So, Roy, do you know where you want to get your core samples?"

"WIGS has identified three sites in the Argentine Pampas, two in Africa and three in India with rankings of eight. If they work out we will look at those with a rank of six to seven."

"The South American sites are in Dobias, two-hundred miles west of Punta Alta; and Rufino, two-hundred miles west of Buenos Aires; and one near

Reconquesta, 400 miles north of Rufino. Reconquesta had the highest rank value."

"Mark can set up there in just a few days. He can put in four holes and get conventional core and run a twelve-foot column of DNAS at each hole."

"After Reconquesta he will move to Rufino and then Dobias."

"In India one is in the Thar Desert near Bikaner, three hundred miles west of Dehli; one near Srinagar in the Jammuand Kashmir, close to the Pakistan border; and one north of Lucknow towards Nepal. Juan and I will start in Lucknow with a drilling crew from GOE and a DNAS operator, then move to Bikaner then Srinagar. It should take about ten days at each of the three sites if we can get in. Bikaner is in the middle of drug traffic lanes and is heavily patrolled. The Srinagar area is in the middle of battling factions between India and Pakistan."

"Africa is also a little problematic. One site is near DeBeers diamond mining country. I doubt we could get in. Depending on success we might get DeBeers to get the core samples for us. The other site is north and east of Allia Bay. At Allia Bay researchers already have hominid species findings of four million years."

"I will review these sites with Conrad to see how they fit his Genome data. He will also have to give Mark the codes for his regressed DNA for the time range."

"Eugene, can you pull some organizational strings and get Conrad assigned to a Wallace Images project so he doesn't have to report to Laney. Laney doesn't have the clearance for what we are doing."

"Is anybody from RENGCA involved?" Eugene asked.

"We don't have anybody from RENGCA. Achmed Rahim is Maximillian's India specialist and is from Patna, southeast of the Lucknow site. Maximillian has lost two people and really can't afford to spare any staff. Let him know that we will bounce any significant anthropological findings in his direction."

"Roy, Achmed is good at cultural subtleties. He can get you around the political and religious barriers you will have in India. India has to be one of the more complex nations. So many people, languages, border disputes. Let me see what I can do about his clearance. I have worked with him. He is okay as far as I am concerned."

"Okay, you break it to Maximillian. We will need at least two weeks for GOE to arrange for equipment to be delivered to Calcutta and drilling pipe and disassembled drilling platforms to be trucked to Lucknow and flown to a site. GOE has surveyors near Mumbai, the old Bombay on the south central coast. They can fly to Lucknow the day after tomorrow and scout a drilling site. Perhaps Achmed could meet them in Lucknow. If his clearance doesn't go through he can leave before the DNAS has to be used. Until he is cleared we are looking for a location for a satellite tracking station."

"I'll get started first thing in the morning," Eugene said as he left the room.

"Jason, set up some time for WIGS mid-morning. When we introduce Achmed to the project we can also run a logistics simulation showing how everything gets moved and when."

"No problem. Roy, does this project have anything to do with the simulation of India moving from the Antarctic to Asia I showed you last week?"

"It turns out it does. India ran into Asia fifty million years ago. We are looking at what happens in the last ten million. Conrad and Mark, coming from two different directions, identified pre-hominid DNA patterns in Triassic deposits. We want to see if we can find other evidence of hominid DNA in the most recent ten-million-year range."

"The interesting thing about the northern edge of India as an evolutionary site..," Roy said as he focused on Lucknow, 100 miles south of the Nepalese border, and zoomed in from a satellite. The Himalayan Mountains to the north took shape. Glaciers and snow-capped peaks rose from the landscape. Muddy threads appeared in the steep valleys of Ghaghara and the Ganges rivers "...is the challenges it presented to adaptation. Granted there was a degree of global uniformity during its 150-million-year journey but the pieces of the Triassic belt we have been following moved through a number of climate changes and magnetic field changes. There were few predators. After India reached Asia and the mountains started developing there were even greater pressures for adaptation. Surviving species of all kinds could adapt or get off the tectonic escalator and migrate."

"Roy, it is one-thirty in the morning. I am going to call it quits for a few hours."

"Good idea, Jason. See you later."

Jason set the parameters for a logistics simulation and turned off the WIGS display.

"The computer will develop a movie of your transportation activity tonight and we can review it later."

The fire bell on the wall of the firehouse clanged and Juan walked up the stairs. "Boss, are you going to sleep all day? I brought coffee from a Seven-Eleven and some donuts."

"Juan, since you got married you sure get up early. Is this your new zest for life or are you escaping?"

"She was starting to talk about going shopping for new furniture. It's starting already."

"Remember, you are going to stay married so you have somebody to come home to. Call and tell her you will pick her up at three. We should be done by then."

"Done with what?" Juan asked as he picked up the phone.

"We are going to go to India for a couple of weeks. WIGS is working out the itinerary and logistics. We have to get over there around eleven o'clock and meet with Achmed Rahim, Conrad and Jason."

"Who is Achmed Rahim?"

"He works for Maximillian and is their expert on India. Achmed grew up not too far from our first drilling site."

"Works for the same group that Henry did and the lady that got killed? Is that a bad luck group?"

"I don't think so, Juan. Let me take a quick shower and we will go."

On the ride past DayBreak Star and to the gates of Wallace Images a half-dozen protesters stood with signs objecting to the unnatural use of whales. The protestors turned their heads and watched as Roy drove by.

"Boss, those guys have been there for weeks. I thought the "Times" retracted or clarified the story that started the problem."

"Some people need a cause even if it is misguided. I have a suspicion that some of them are paid to be here to keep track of who goes in and out. It is a good cover for spying. They have seen us before as regulars. They paid a lot more attention the first time Mark came in."

"Who does that, the spying?"

"All sorts of groups."

WIGS was expanded to the largest size, some thirty feet in diameter. India was in the foreground. A red circle enclosed an area above Lucknow. A second circle enclosed Calcutta. A third circle enclosed Kuala Lumpur near the tip of the Malaysian Peninsula. A red line connected Calcutta with Lucknow. A dotted blue line went north from Lucknow across the Ghaghara River.

"GOE has a large exploration project going on outside of Kuala Lumpur," Jason said. He looked at the red circle and pushed the highlight button on his console. The circled area flashed. "As we speak, drilling equipment is being loaded onto a freighter in Kuala Lumpur, bound for Calcutta. It leaves port in six hours. Mark has coordinated the equipment requirements with his staff."

Jason said, "Watch this." He pressed the button labeled "satellite" and the "zoom" button. A flat panel appeared in front of WIGS showing the Malay Peninsula growing larger. After a few seconds he had zoomed onto the docks. A crane could be seen lifting long wooden boxes labeled *Drill Rod* onto the deck of a rusting freighter. The view was held for a minute and then faded.

"The freighter will reach port day after tomorrow," Jason said. "The rod, the towers, engines, cable, fuel, water pumps, water tanks and miscellaneous equipment will be loaded onto several flatbeds and taken north of Lucknow. That should take three more days."

"Are there any problems we should know about?" Roy asked.

Jason pushed a button. "The shaded areas along the route are where there is a military presence and political unrest." The shaded area grew brighter then returned to its original level of illumination. "The Department of State has been notified of our passage through these areas and the Indian government is being asked to provide safe passage. GOE has some operatives watching."

"A helicopter will take the survey staff and equipment from Kuala Lumpur in five days and meet the trucks at the transition site. From there all the equipment will be carried to the drill site by helicopter."

"Do they know exactly where they are going?" Achmed asked.

"Not really. The geologists can identify candidate-drilling sites based on topography. You, Roy and Juan are going to leave tonight to meet them. Your flights have been booked to Delhi northwest of Lucknow and quasi-commercial jet helicopters will take you from there to the general area." Jason evoked the satellite linkage and zoomed in on a barren rock and sand covered landscape cut by four-thousand-foot-deep gorges. The rivers cut through the rock as the mountains rose.

When the view was three miles above the surface, tents from a nomadic group could be seen to the east.

"We have watched the area for a while, Jason said, and from time to time dust clouds appear on the eastern and northern boundaries. We have not really spent the time to figure out if winds, animals or vehicles cause the dust. Just like the rest of India, there are people everywhere. The reason you have to go there is to determine whether or not the wandering groups pose any threat to a smooth drilling activity."

"Jason," Roy said, "that is a great way to plan trips."

"Jason, Sahib, please," Achmed interrupted, "Would it be possible to look at the home of my parents?"

"Sure, Achmed. Press the button labeled Retina. A series of calibration circles of different colors will appear. As soon as you have focused on a circle push the Retina button. After a while a calibrated sign will appear."

Achmed responded to the calibration spots in a few seconds. "Now what?"

"Look at where you think your parents home is and hold down the zoom-in button. The background will adjust and try to follow your eyes as you move in."

"Praise Allah," Achmed said, "and those who learned to use what he has given. Thank you, Sahib Jason. Look there. There is the house I was born in. I want to wave but they could not see me, could they?"

The scene was a small white one-story brick dwelling with a bricked in garden the size of the house. As

Achmed zoomed out, his parent's house disappeared in the maze of white houses and gardens of the same size.

"Jason," Roy asked, "Has Mark set up their first site yet?"

Jason pressed his retina button and looked at the western horizon of the globe. The earth turned until he could focus on South America, the Pampas region and finally on a blinking dot. The globe was still turning as he zoomed in on four trucks and two helicopters.

"They are there and it looks like a coffee break."

Roy was on the phone while Jason spoke. "Patch me through to Mark."

"Mark, tell the crew to wave to the great eye in the sky."

Jason laughed, "Look at that, they are waving."

"Mark, tell them they look great. When do you think you will put in your first hole?"

"Two days," Mark said.

"Sounds good, Mark," Roy said. "Juan, Achmed and I are leaving in the morning. We should be on site north of Lucknow, India, day after tomorrow given the time changes. Talk to you later." Roy placed the telephone in its cradle.

"He says hi to everyone," Roy said. "Since we have our marching orders let's clean up our desks and get ready to go."

"Achmed," Roy said, "a Wallace Images car will pick you up in the morning around four. See you at the airport."

"Juan, have a good time shopping. Why don't you crash at my place tonight? Use the downstairs bedroom. It will help the logistics but not necessarily the marriage."

CHAPTER 13
PAMPAS

Five silver festooned gauchos slowly moved their horses toward the small clutch of tents. Mark had noticed them half-an-hour before working their way closer. For the past week the horsemen had blended in to the horizon. They first appeared on the third day of drilling at the first hole. Mark thought it would be impossible not to be noticed. All the water for the drilling tower had to be flown in by helicopter.

During daylight while the four-man crew lowered and retracted drill rod, the helicopter flew to the Parana River with a large bucket with a movable bottom. Hovering over the river, the helicopter would lower the bucket with the bottom open. When the bucket was raised the bottom would close and trap five hundred gallons of water. Pits had been dug two hundred feet east of the drill tower and lined with treated nylon tarps forming small reservoirs. The bucket bottom opened when set on a spillway that fed into the reservoirs called hog troughs. PVC pipe connected the reservoirs to the drilling tower.

Water was essential to drilling. It was pumped to the bottom of the drill hole to cool the cutting tools that chewed and ground at the rock below. The drilling supervisor sampled the mud that rose from the hole. He rubbed it between his fingers, looked at it, and smelled it. From the color and texture he knew how many thousands of years they had penetrated.

The horses stopped two hundred feet west of the tower. The gauchos watched silently. Neither horse nor rider moved when the helicopter thundered down four hundred feet away.

Carlos Vega, one of the rod men on the drill, looked at Martin Reyles, his co-worker and pointed with his eyes toward the horses. "Who are they?"

"Keep working," Martin said. "During our break last night Mark had told us not to pay attention to the gauchos if they came into camp. The owner of the land is very wealthy. Wheat is his primary agricultural product. His hobby is breeding Black Angus cattle. Can you believe it, as a hobby, he has one of the largest Black Angus cattle herds in Argentina. For show he had his gauchos dress to fit the mid-18th to mid-19th century romantic notion of the gauchos. Silver ornaments on the saddles and clothing, bolas instead of lariats. They were like a working Buffalo Bill Western show but for real. We aren't supposed to do anything that might be considered hostile or threatening."

The Gauchos watched the rod crew add a section of drill pipe to the drill stem. Carlos swung a choke collar around the exposed section of the stem and pulled down on a large handle that locked the collar to the drill stem at the top of the hole. Martin unscrewed the connector, attaching the hoisting cable to the top section of rod. He pulled the connector to a twenty-five foot piece of rod on the ground. He attached the connector to the rod, raised his right arm and pointed his index finger up, moving it in a circle. Dandin Capricho, operating the engine, raised the piece of rod and swung it over the top of the stem. Carlos grabbed the moving pipe and guided it over the top of the drill stem. Martin connected it to the drill stem. Carlos signaled to Dandin the connection had been made. Martin released the securing collar and engaged the torque drive to turn the long stem. The adding of a new section of drill rod to the top of the growing stem was a choreographed ballet of muscle, grease, water and machine. From the instant the torque drive was released and the stem clamped, to the time the drive was engaged again, there were no wasted movements. Everybody knew exactly how far to reach, what to grasp, how hard to pull and push and how to get their fingers out of the way of swinging bone crushing metal.

With the gauchos watching, Martin and Carlos exaggerated their movements and added a few flourishes to their signals. The gauchos did not change their expressions or move. "Tough crowd," Martin said.

If the grit coming out of the hole grew too fine, the supervisor knew the bit was wearing and would have to be replaced. Replacing the bit meant that the entire length of the drill stem had to be disassembled, twenty-five feet at a time. Pulling a bit from a thousand foot hole meant pulling up the stem so the second piece of rod could be secured. Once secured, it had to be uncoupled from the first piece with large wrenches. The top piece would be lowered onto a rack and disconnected from the hauling cable. The cable had to be connected to the piece of rod clamped at the top of the hole and the entire stem raised twenty-five feet and secured so the top piece of rod could be removed. For a five-hundred-foot stem the process had to be repeated twenty times without error to avoid injury to operators or damage to the equipment. If the stem is dropped into the hole it might be impossible to retract it and a new hole would have to be started.

Once the last piece of rod is hauled up a new bit is added. Then the process of connecting all twenty sections together has to be started. At times after retracting a long stem and reassembling the stem the crew would collapse from exhaustion, unable to move.

There were two crews. One hauled rod, one slept. The only time there was a break in the routine was for meals or moving to a new site.

After watching for an hour at the short distance, one horseman nudged his steed forward the length of the horse. Mark looked up, raised his right hand in rec-

PAMPAS

ognition, and walked to the horseman. The crew kept working.

The horseman spoke Spanish and asked if his master, the owner of the land had given permission. Mark smiled, and never taking his eyes from those of the horseman, pulled a leather wallet from his shirt pocket. It had a brand on it, the same as on all the horses. He handed it to the Gaucho. The horseman opened the wallet, unfolded a piece of parchment, reviewed it, returned it to the wallet and handed it back to Mark. Mark said, in Spanish, "Have a nice day." The horseman straightened, smiled and backed his horse to be in line with the others. All the horses turned in unison and the Gauchos left, first in a slow trot then a full gallop.

"Now that is class," Mark said aloud.

"Mark, how deep do we have to go on this hole?" asked Kyle the drilling supervisor. They were at the dinner table. Meals were served in twelve-by-eight tents with enough room for a three-by-eight-foot table, benches, a wood stove adapted to burn fuel oil, a cabinet for storing cooking supplies and condiments.

"I doubt we will go more that six hundred feet. That last one was only 200 feet. Where are we now?"

"Only at one-hundred fifty. Six rods. It is still easy going. The sod under this grass is deep, and then there is a little layer of basalt and cemented ash. What exactly are we looking for, oil?"

"No, oil would really screw this trip up. No, looking at fossil contents and a place to put in a stable platform for a deep space communication station."

"Tomorrow when you get to two hundred feet I want to drop the instrument package. That means you will have to pull the stem. Depending on what we find we might move on."

"Whoa." Said Ramirez Lozana, a new drill rod puller, as rings started forming in his coffee cup and silverware rattled. The table lurched and glasses of water spilled. The kerosene lantern hanging from the ridge board of the framed tent on a coat hanger hook started swinging.

"Earthquake." Kyle uttered the obvious. "You'll get used to them."

"That was a pretty good one," Mark said. "I'm going to find out where it was located."

Mark went to the tent that served as an office, opened his laptop computer and called Wallace Images on a cell phone with a satellite pickup. The number connected to Jason's office. As soon as Jason answered, the laptop had finished the booting sequence.

"Good evening, Mark," Jason said. "You want to know about the earthquake, right?"

"Hi Jason, have you taken up mind reading?"

"Not quite, but I figured you would be interested in the quake that hit you. It was a bit of a surprise to John Wellington, our geophysicist in charge of earthquakes. He was expecting something from your volcano but not the quake. It was 7.6 on the Richter scale. The epicenter is below the volcano forty miles from the canyons. WIGS is showing massive destruction in the villages along the southern Andes. Lots of landslides. We can still see some bridges collapsing."

"Mark, you had better check back with me in an hour or so to see if we can learn anything more about the volcanic activity above the canyons."

"Thanks, Jason. Can you patch me through to Roy?"

"Roy."

"Hi, Roy," Mark said, "Is it time to get up in India?"

"Almost," Roy grunted. "I think it's starting to get light outside." Roy rolled over on his canvas cot and pulled back the flap to his tent. "Yeh, it will get light in a couple of hours. How are you doing, Mark?"

Mark gave Roy a quick summary. "We had some positive flashes at 120, 150 and 185 feet in the first hole. We have a strong flash at 90 feet in the hole we are in. I will scan the hole again at 150 feet. That will probably take six more hours of drilling."

"My reason for calling," Mark said, "is there has been a sizeable quake below the volcano above the canyons. Jason says it will take a little time to get a fix on the impact on the volcano's scheduled eruption."

Mark waited to let Roy wake up. "By the way, how are you doing? We haven't talked since you started lifting gear to your drill site. Any signs?"

"Oh, we are having a ball. It has been slower than expected. The local nomads like to use our water buckets for target practice. Right now we are on a ridge and exposed. The water has to come up from the river a thousand feet below. We have had some weak flashes at 600 feet. The WIGS process for selecting highly probable locations didn't have enough input data on accessibility. I am not sure how much longer I am going to stay at this hole. I was thinking about moving to a drill site on the other side of the river gorge tomorrow."

"Mark, have you ever scanned on a fly-by?"

"Not really. We did a little with the third helicopter we lost in the canyon. Walt Woltowski tried scanning the walls as they descended. They crashed before we found out if the technique works. We just got around to running some simple tests. Why do you ask?"

"Yesterday I was in the helicopter on a water run down to the river. I had DNAS pointing at the sides of the gorge as we went down. DNAS started flashing 190 feet below the ridgeline. I planned to go back today and just scan the slopes on both sides. The river has cut through the Triassic belt and eroded away the highly probable site."

"If you get more signs on the slopes you might consider hydraulic mining, sluice the slopes and wash all the bones into a net at the bottom. It will make a great employment program for museum types. They can figure out where all the bones go."

"I never did understand your sense of humor. Wouldn't work anyway. We are looking for a stable site on which to put a solid radio telescope platform. It wouldn't wash. Ha ha!"

"Roy, what do you want to do if the volcano eruption schedule moves up?

"I'll pack up here in India and get back to your location in Punta Alta. Maybe you should think about trenching out your best hot spot. Get a bulldozer in there. Officially you will be doing soil testing for a very heavy platform. You get your next DNAS readings from inside the hole and find out what Jason has learned. Then get back to me."

"Talk to you later, Roy."

"Ralph, I want to drop to the river, staying as close to the slope as possible."

Ralph Haussman, the pilot, moved the helicopter sideways toward the crumbling barren fifty-degree slope. Roy held the DNAS in his lap pointed at the slope. He watched the scintillation screen and the out-cropping they slowly moved past. The blades of the he-licopter occasionally stirred up so much dust that Ralph had to back away. The downdraft of the blades eroded the ancient deposits that had weathered in the continu-ous cycles of freezing and thawing at 11,000 feet. They were in the low-lying foothills of the Himalayas, one hundred fifty miles from south of Katmandu, in Asia. To the north the mountains grew higher and higher until they reached 27,000 and 28,000 feet.

The downdraft dislodged rocks that left a trail of dust as they rolled and bounced down the slope dislodg-ing other rocks until small avalanches fanned out across the slope.

"This stuff is as unstable as it can get." Ralph shouted over the noise that echoed back from the slope.

"Just keep it as close as you can," Roy answered. "You're the pilot. Use your judgment but keep me as close as you can."

A scintillation flash filled the screen. Roy was mesmerized. "Wait. Record the GPS location. Move upstream a little. Another hundred feet."

The flashing was continuous.

"Keep going upstream until I say stop."

After two hundred yards the intensity of the flashes decreased and finally ceased.

"Ralph, go back to where we started and go downstream."

The flashing increased as they retraced their path to the spot where the scintillation had started. The helicopter continued downstream another hundred yards before the screen blanked out.

To Roy's right was a ninety-foot-high gray weathered outcropping under a dull red tinted brown layer of basalt, volcanic rock that had been deposited in Asia before India tried to slide under. He was looking at a portion of the contact zone between two continents.

"Go to the other side of the gorge. Try to find this formation."

Ralph nodded and he turned to the left. The helicopter dropped, then started climbing in shallow spirals like birds following a thermal current.

"Mr. Graham, I can't find any more of that gray layer."

Roy had Ralph go from the top of the higher northern slope then slowly descend to the river four thousand feet below. At the bottom the brown muddy torrents of the river carried pulverized boulders toward the Ganges. They returned to the gray layer on the south side.

"I need some of that rock," Roy said.

Ralph shook his head. "No place to land."

Roy looked around in the helicopter. "Let me use that rope. I'll climb down eighty feet or so. That should give you enough clearance if you put me at the top edge of the gray layer."

"I can't let you do that. It would be suicide."

"No problem, I do it all the time," Roy said. "In my dreams.

Look, Ralph, I need a sample of that rock. It would not be possible to go down that slope on foot. We have to do it from here."

Roy climbed into the back of the helicopter. He uncoiled a climbing rope and tied one end to a pilot-controlled-hook on the ceiling. Before lowering the rope out over the skid he tied a figure eight knot at the loose end. He took a climbing harness, a rappelling ring and two jumars from his pack. He would use the rappelling ring to lower himself eighty feet and then use the jumars or ascenders to climb back up that rope. He attached half a dozen canvas rock sample bags to his harness. Ralph handed him a helmet with a radio built in.

"Ralph," he said.

"Loud and clear."

"I'll go down and climb back. If I have any trouble, go to the top and drop me on the ridge and release the rope."

Ralph raised a fist and extended thumb.

Roy climbed out on the skid, looked down three thousand feet and dropped off as gently as he could. The river had cut down through the weak contact zone forming the valley as the plateau rose and tilted upward. He could feel the rope sliding through his gloves but couldn't hear it. His helmet and the noise of the helicopter drowned out all sensations. "Ugh! I am not used to this," he thought as a mild jolt of adrenaline surged though his system.

Ralph held the helicopter steady.

"Okay Ralph, I am at eighty feet. Can you move me over?" Hanging from the eleven-millimeter rope Roy focused on the gray outcropping fifty feet in front of him. "More."

"Roy, it is too steep here. You will have go further down on the rope. I am going to climb up to where I can get over the outcrop. Then you drop down."

Roy watched the slope as he rose fifty feet and moved over the top edge of the rock he was after. The helicopter stopped rising.

"Okay Roy, go on down."

Roy let the rope slide though the rappel ring. The elasticity of the rope added a bouncing motion to his descent. The downdraft was blowing dust and small rocks onto him and he was starting to spin slowly. As he turned to face the rock the grit peppered the facemask of his helmet and stung his neck and wrists.

At 130 feet below the helicopter, he touched the rock and stopped the spinning. Volcanic ash, he thought. Roy had left the DNAS in the helicopter and wasn't sure where to take samples. He found the pick of his hammer would sink into the relatively soft rock. When he swung the hammer hard into the rock, he bounced on the rope. He knocked away some outer layers to get back to unweathered rock and put some fist-sized samples in the bags hanging on his belt. He lowered himself another ten feet. He could see the knot on the end of the rope ten feet below him.

He hacked away at the weathered face of a protruding ledge. It popped off. A round smooth concave lens of white rock appeared. It was the top of a skull. He froze, staring at the skullcap. Adrenaline jolted his elbows and knees. His mind was snapping pictures of the rock, the finest details of rock became vivid. A vertical crack to the right of the skull revealed itself. Another hairline crack angled to the left from above the skull and curved over to the vertical crack.

"Roy, how are you doing? Roy? Hey Roy, what's the problem? I am going to take you up."

Ralph's voice registered with Roy. "No, do not move. I am okay. I just found something and am trying to figure how to get it out. Raise me about two feet. Ralph, you are a fantastic pilot. Hold it."

"Ralph, I want to blast my way in. Move upstream about five feet."

Roy fumbled under his climbing harness to get at his pistol holster. Ralph and Roy had started carrying weapons when they were being shot at. He pulled out his .44 magnum and took aim at a spot four inches above the angled crack. He pulled the trigger and could not see what happened. The recoil of the pistol spun him like a top.

"Into the rock," he yelled. "Push me into the rock."

Ralph moved Roy gently into the cliff.

A large chunk of rock had been blown away from the left side of the skullcap. A shoulder bone appeared on the left. "Okay Ralph, I need to take another shot. Ease me out. When I shoot take me back into the wall."

"Okay."

Roy took aim to the right of the vertical crack. He pulled the trigger and felt himself slam into the wall.

"That's close enough, Ralph. Thank you. Move me downstream three feet."

Roy looked at a complete skeleton on its back down to the waist. Its arms were crossed over the chest. "Ralph, this is going to get tricky. I want to extract a rather large sample. It will be too big to put into a bag. I will have to hang on to it and you can take me to the top."

Roy pushed against the matrix holding the skull and shoulders. A rectangular block of the rock moved slightly. Using his hammer he removed crumbling material from under the skull's matrix. A large piece of supporting rock popped out. The top half of the skeleton shifted forward and slid toward the abyss in front of it. Roy's motion swinging the hammer and his sudden movement when the rock fell from under the skeleton started him bouncing on the rope away from the cliff.

"In." He yelled. Ralph shifted the helicopter and the rope followed. Roy slammed into the wall, grabbing at the skull. The matrix started to slide out of the wall where it had been entombed for ten million years. Frantically Roy tried to push his knee up against the skull and get his arms around the middle of the slab that was tilting away from the cliff. "Down, down, down," He yelled.

Ralph had been watching Roy from a mirror and could see what was happening with the rock. He saw the skull slide into Roy's lap upside down. Roy was grabbing at the arms as the rock fell away from the cliff. If he could descend fast enough maybe Roy would have a fraction of a second more to secure it.

It was a weightless free fall. For a fraction of a second Roy dropped along with the ten million-year-old man. The body and rock twisted. Roy grabbed a hand at the side of the rock and pulled the rock into his chest.

Ralph slowed the descent of the helicopter to avoid running his blades into the steep slope. Roy and the hundred-pound rock continued to drop, stretching out the elastic line to its limit. It snapped back, obeying the laws of physics, accelerating Roy upward. The force ripped the matrix from him taking a glove, a shirtsleeve, pant leg and half his climbing harness. He hung by one leg and a safety loop attached to his chest harness and the rappel ring, which had been shoved down to the end of the rope and jammed on the knot. He watched in horror as the skull smiling back at him dropped to the river below.

He looked up when he felt the tug of the rope as Ralph took the helicopter to the top of the gorge. It took several seconds for him to realize he was holding the skeleton's hand. He looked at the hand in his. "Glad to meet you."

CHAPTER 14
DIGGING

Ralph didn't stop at the top of the gorge. He flew past the drilling platform to the campsite. The drillers saw Roy dangling sideways from the end of 150 feet of rope. They secured the pipe stem and ran toward camp. Achmed and Juan emerged from the tents as Ralph arrived above them and lowered Roy. Juan grabbed Roy's left foot and guided him to the ground. Achmed, standing off to the side, signaled that Roy was down. Ralph released the rope from the hook on the ceiling of the helicopter. It fell on the driller's bunk tent. The rope weighed only eight pounds but it made a lot of noise hitting the tent made from canvas stretched over a wood frame.

Roy was sitting up when the startled drillers who were sleeping in the tent when the rope fell, darted out in their underwear. "Now that is what I call a reception." The others arrived. Ralph had landed the helicopter and ran to Roy.

"That is the last time I let you jump out of my helicopter," he said. "You could have been killed. Who was that that fell into the river?"

"Uncle Charlie," Roy said smiling at Achmed.

"Roy, you are covered in blood, you're a mess," Juan said as he reached down to help Roy up. He saw the hand Roy was holding. "My god, you ripped the skin off your arm."

One of the drillers saw the hand and heard Juan and gagged and threw up.

"I am okay." Roy said as he stood hopping onto one foot. He held out the hand. "It is a piece of skeleton we found in the gorge." Roy looked at Ralph and shook his head slightly. Ralph understood that he wasn't to say anything about the skeleton.

"Who is it?" Achmed asked.

"Has to be a local. Died some time ago."

One of the drillers said, "Damn border disputes. Everybody is shooting at everybody else. It's a wonder one of us hasn't been hit. Bullets were ricocheting off the water bucket and drill pipe. I'll be glad when we get out of here."

"Juan, help me to my tent. I need a few bandages, shirt and pants and I have to contact Mark. Can you raise him while I change?"

As Roy limped to his tent he handed Juan the hand. "Secure this. For the moment it is the most valuable thing on the planet. Nobody, but nobody, is to know that it is anything other than a local that got shot last year. Ask Ralph to come over here."

"Ralph, you did a fantastic job. I'm sorry I put you at risk. The hand that I found, and the rest that got lost, came from the riverbed. Okay?"

"Understood."

"Thanks."

"Mark. Did you shoot the new hole? You did?"
Mark explained that the DNAS he lowered into the new hole registered a very strong signal.

"What is the status of the volcano?"

"Jason said John Wellington has moved up the estimated eruption to four to five weeks maximum."

"Mark, stop the drilling and get a bulldozer on site. Dig and try to locate the source of your scintillation. I'll bag the operation here. The drilling crew can return to Kuala Lumpur. Achmed will head back to Wallace Images with a possible side trip to visit his parents. They live nearby."

"What about the rest of your drilling?"

"Mark, we don't need to drill any more, at least not now."

"You found something?"

"Unimaginable, but I dropped it into the river."

"What? How could you?"

"Clumsy I guess. I'll see you in a couple of days. See what you can dig up."

"Achmed, Juan and I have to go visit Mark and you are going back to Wallace Images. If you want, Ralph can drop you off in Patna at your parents for a couple of days. He can pick you up on his last trip out after the drill site has been cleared."

"I cannot imagine anything more wonderful. How can I ever repay you?

"Easy, never mention that you have ever been here. You came to India to visit your parents, that's all."

"I think I understand. Thank you."

"Hello Commandante," Roy said after he and Juan landed at the Punta Alta airport. He handed the local official a box of Cuban cigars. The pilot of the private GOE jet had given Roy the box indicating they were the Commandante's favorite and that GOE always included a note of appreciation in the box.

The Commandante opened the box. "They always smell so good when the box is first opened." He sniffed the contents and reached to the bottom to rub a crisp thousand-dollar bill between his thumb and index finger. "So good." He repeated.

As if on cue a helicopter landed and Mark climbed out. "Commandante, so good to see you," he said and shook hands. "Roy, Juan, let's go. Goodbye, Commandante," he shook hands with the local official again.

Roy and Juan climbed into the back of the helicopter, Mark into the co-pilot's seat. "That was a full minute on the ground, Mark," Roy chuckled. "We have to work on your pit stop time. You didn't even clean the windshield."

"What did you find in India?" Mark asked.

"I had a whole, intact skeleton and dropped it. I've set science back a generation."

"Don't worry; I can make up for it." Mark had a grin that cracked his sunburned face. "Just wait."

"So," Roy said, "the concept that you and Conrad put together about pre-hominid DNA moving along on the Triassic belt is working out. Fantastic. Is the world ready for you guys?"

"They can never know, at least that GOE is involved." Mark said.

"Two things about the India site," Roy said after a few minutes. "I think it demonstrates the idea that man evolved in more than one place. Second, I did manage to hang on to a hand from the skeleton I dropped. We can compare the DNA to your find."

The helicopter circled the excavation site. The drilling tower had been disassembled and the drill rod lay stacked south of the earth works. Stakes with red, blue and yellow plastic tape marked the boundary of a rectangular area one hundred feet square. A bulldozer had removed twenty feet of the entire rectangular surface. A series of terraces had been cut to a depth of sixty-seven feet on the West end. At thirty feet there was a ten-foot layer of red volcanic rock. At forty feet there was a twelve-foot layer of peat suggesting a low swampy history, overlaying another ten-foot basalt layer. The bottom layer of the terracing was hardened dark gray volcanic ash.

When they landed Mark, Juan and Roy climbed down to the deepest level. Mark carried his DNAS and focused on the wall of the next highest step under a stake with a blue ribbon. The scintillation screen saturated with flashing. Scintillation was still strong at the base of trenching.

"That is the strength of the signal I had in the gorge. Your source is no more than twelve inches in."

"You are right. I ran a small probe in and tapped what might have been bone. We ran an ultra-sound scan and outlined what is probably a teenager. I know there are more bones under here but I didn't find anything until you got here. Between your find in India and what is under here, what do you want to do?"

"Let's pull the bulldozer down here and nudge up against the area of the skeleton. Use a hammer to remove the immediate cover so that it looks like the covering on the skeleton sloughed off. The foreman will see the skeleton before the blade can do any damage. The foreman stops the digging until an anthropologist arrives and verifies what has been found. The anthropologist gets to claim the find, take the credit, etc."

"It works for me."

"How about you, Juan," Roy asks, "anything to add?"

"Who is the supervisor?"

"Mike Swersey."

"Why don't you call him down here, start the bulldozer and make your cut. By the time he gets down here I can have the head exposed."

"Mike," Mark clicked his radio transmitter. "Mike come on down here. I want to show these guys how we cut a terrace."

"Be right down."

Juan picked away at the soft rock until a small section crumbled revealing the top of a skull.

"God that looks familiar," Roy said.

Mark moved the bulldozer forward, the blade cutting six inches into the wall. He moved until Juan signaled a stop. Juan and Roy packed rock up against the skull.

"Hey Mark, you're not supposed to be cutting without a supervisor," Mike shouted running and jumping from one terrace level to another. "Christ, if I did that you'd have my ass hauled across the Pampas by the Gauchos."

"Sorry, Mike. I got carried away talking to my friends. I haven't done anything yet. Let's run ahead a little."

"Okay. Take it easy."

Mark increased the rpm's of the engine and slowly let out the clutch. The blade cut into the bank and knocked away the filler that had been packed around the skull. Mike jumped in front of the advancing blade yelling for Mark to stop.

"What the hell is that?" Mike asked.

Roy opened his multi-tooled pocketknife to a leather punch and picked away the rock around the skull.

"Everybody out of the pit," Mike said. "When we find bones, especially further down, we have to bring in an anthropologist. There are more damn lawsuits over old bones. Anybody know a good anthropologist?"

"There is a guy up in Seattle at a group called RENGCA Works with people all around the world," Roy said.

"What do you think Mark, should we call him or get somebody from one of the local Universities?"

"I think the RENGCA group sounds best. Can you contact him, Roy?"

"I'll try. Let's go get your phone."

"Maximillian, how are you?"

"Roy, where are you calling from? Are you still in India? How is Achmed doing?"

"Achmed is visiting his parents in Patna. I am in South America visiting my friend Mark. He is on a site survey project for the UN trying to identify a location for a large space telescope, the effort Achmed is working on. A bulldozer just uncovered some bones. It looks like they might be old. We were wondering if you could come down and take a look at them."

"You mean right now?"

"The longer they have to wait the more it costs them. Jet fuel is cheap."

"You have to be kidding, but I'll do it. Where do I go?"

"Mark, give him the particulars," Roy said handing him the phone."

"Maximillian Schnell, we met several weeks ago. It is good to talk again. Rather than you trying to figure out where to go we'll send a car to pick you up. The driver will take to you to the old Boeing field on East Marginal Way. He should be at your office in twenty minutes.

"I have to pack."

"Just tell the driver your clothing sizes and they will have something for you when you get here. Have an enjoyable trip. See you tomorrow."

"You know, Mark, I think you just made his day."

"What happens," Mark responded, "when he finds a ten-million year old man?"

"What about the hand?" Juan asked.

"He is not going to find that until next year," Roy answered.

"I don't understand you two." Juan shook his head.

Dirt started trickling down the faces of the terraces and stopped. A few seconds later more dirt started trickling down. This time there was enough to create little dust clouds.

"Boss, I think I have felt this before. What is going to happen?"

The ground heaved and rolled like a large ocean swell. Juan fell down. Roy staggered. Mark leaned against the bulldozer. Dirt slid down each terrace and sloughed into the bottom. Roy lifted Juan and put him on the bulldozer and climbed onto it himself. Mark had already climbed to the roof of the cab and helped Juan as dirt cascaded down and filled the bottom eight feet of the pit.

"Looks like Max will have to dig for his prize," Mark said. "Roy, we had better check with Jason. Give you odds we have to get the other captives out of the canyons. Let's get up to my tent, get some bourbon, and figure what to do."

Roy stepped off of the roof of the bulldozer onto the slope that had buried the large piece of machinery. He tested with one foot, pushing down to see if the soil would compact and hold his weight.

"We can climb up the slope to the top terrace the same way we would hiking up a snow slope. Use the rest step."

Roy pushed his right foot down on the slope in front of him and rested on his left leg. Then he leaned forward putting pressure on the right foot and stood up. At the same time he transferred weight to his right foot he pushed his left foot forward and pushed it down onto the loose soil. By first pushing down before transferring all of his weight to a foot the soil compacted and held him instead of slipping out from under him.

They slowly made their way to the top. The supervisor and the rest of the crew had run to the edge of the large pit expecting to have to dig out three bodies. When they saw Mark, Roy and Juan they let out a cheer.

"Thanks for your concern, guys," Mark said as he, Roy and Juan went to Mark's tent.

Roy opened his laptop and connected to WIGS remotely and accessed the satellite view of the canyon. Several places along the rims of the four canyons had been cracked. Large sections had split off and fallen to the floors, snagging the nets below them. For the first time Roy could see movement deep in the canyons.

"Not all the nets are torn," he said while Mark and Juan looked over his shoulder. "These blank, out-of-focus areas are nets. Notice, in each case, the valley is wider. Those must be the gardens."

"Look at those guys go," Juan pointed to Mapinguari climbing cracks carrying lines to haul nets. "What's that up there? Top and left in the cave opening."

"Looks like a harpoon gun sticking out of the cave. There is a big rock at the edge of the opening."

"There are more of those things climbing around on a net on the other side of the canyon. That net is just hanging there."

"You have a good eye, Juan," Roy said. "Oh, oh, look at that."

A boulder four feet in diameter dropped from the cave opening from under the harpoon gun. The boulder had a hole drilled through and was tethered to a line that ran over a pulley under the barrel of the harpoon gun. The boulder fell seventy feet and the line went taught. The boulder continued to fall. The line was tied to the back end of a cradle that traveled along the barrel of the gun. As the rock accelerated down the side of the cliff the large spear riding on the cradle accelerated toward the opening of the lava tube.

"So that is how they do it," Mark murmured as the cradle slammed to a halt at the opening of the cave and the spear continued its ballistic trajectory across the canyon. "They are using a gravity catapult to launch a line across the canyon that is half a mile wide. There, the missile just tangled in the netting on the other side. The Mapinguari are climbing down to it, to secure the haul line it carried."

"I bet that is how they netted our helicopters," Mark said. "They used catapults to throw the nets after the helicopters had dropped below the caves."

"This Stone Age crowd keeps amazing me," said Roy. "It is not going to be easy to get the captives out. We have to get rid of the nets. As soon as the nets are gone the Mapinguari are going to swarm all over the place. We have already seen that they throw spears that will slice through light metal and flack jackets."

"What are all the things that have to be done?" Mark uncovered a white slate slightly larger than a piece of notebook paper and took a pencil from his shirt pocket. "First, we need to get rid of the nets," he wrote what he was saying. "Second, we need to incapacitate the Mapinguari but not kill them."

Roy and Juan nodded agreement.

"Third, we need to transport the people in the gardens to the surface and protect them during the trip."

"Fourth, we need to remove them from the surface while we go to the next canyon."

"Even if we burn the nets," Roy added, "we still can't be sure they won't shoot down a chopper with one of those harpoons or net it. All getting rid of the nets does is give a us a view."

Juan took a sip of bourbon. "How fast can they replace the nets and how many nets can they replace in, say, two days or three?"

"What are you thinking, Juan?"

"You know, Boss, that every time we get ready to go on a trip you keeping adding people. I never have enough of a stockpile of equipment and get delayed in what I am doing running down to REI to buy new stuff."

"Are you suggesting we keep burning them out until they run out of nets and have to make more?"

"That is what I am suggesting."

"What will happen to the captives during that time period?"

"The wolf is coming." Juan laughed.

"Mark, you had better put the bourbon away. Juan has had enough but is coming up with good ideas. If we burn the nets and nothing happens they drop their guard and put the captives back into the gardens without the nets. Also, if they run out of nets they might still need to have the gardening continue. They probably would increase the number of sentries."

"We can't chance putting a helicopter in there," Marc said.

"We need a bath."

"Juan I think you are drunk," Roy took Juan's cup and tossed the remainder of his bourbon out of the tent.

"Oh great," Mark said. "Drunk scorpions."

"Not a bath to get clean in, a bathysphere."

Mark looked at Roy. "The bathysphere was William Beebee's submersible used to go to the deepest part of the Pacific, in the Marianne Trench."

"Juan, you have done it again." Roy patted Juan on the back.

"We don't go into the canyon with the helicopters. We lower a cage to the bottom. Can you get two thousand feet of cable on reel and lift ten to twelve people?"

"I think so. We have mine shafts deeper than that and we take the cable to the mines with our cargo choppers."

"Will that operate at 15,000 feet?"

"A couple of our new ones do, yeah."

"Like shooting fish in a barrel," were the last words Juan muttered before he fell asleep.

"Even drunk and asleep he has insight." Roy took Mark's tablet and made a sketch of a small rectangular structure with jets on the side.

"We need a small tempered steel carriage that will hold ten to twelve people that can be lowered."

"What are the devices on the sides."

"Thrusters, small jets that can be used to stabilize the carriage and keep it from spinning. They can be controlled automatically with gyroscopic sensors and manually from inside the helicopter." As Roy talked, he sketched a steel walled shack with hinge pin joints connecting the sides, floor and roof.

"I can get the welders in our shop in Punta Alta working on that before we go to bed."

"The last problem, Roy, is what is to keep the sentries from killing the captives if they think they will lose them anyway?"

"We will have to try to tranquilize them. Put sharp shooters along the rim with smart bullets loaded with tranquilizer."

"Smart bullets?"

"Some new Pandora Box devices. The General has wanted to find an opportunity to try them out in the field. I'll call him after you get the cages started."

"How many cages do we need?"

"A minimum of two. I think we have to put two down at the same time or the second immediately after the first takes off. We have to minimize the response time of the Mapinguari once they know something is happening. As soon as the first one gets to the top of the canyon, the people have to be removed and the cage dropped into the next canyon."

"Roy, remember on our trip into the canyon and out? By the time we were a few miles downstream they had massed in large numbers. Let's assume they all didn't come from the first canyon but word spread to the other canyons. How did they communicate?"

"That has bothered me. The only thing I can think of is the Hawk that ripped my wet suit. It carried off a good size piece of neoprene. Maybe it was the messenger."

"Do we tranquilize anything that flies?"

"Or walks. Remember the monks."

CHAPTER 15
DIARY

"Mark, when will the welders finish the flying houses?"

"Chuck, the GOE foreman in Punta Alta, said it will take three days to do the welding and another to temper and harden the surfaces on the sides. He is also locating a couple of large cable reels that will hold a couple thousand feet of cable. He thinks there is one in Bogota and one in Lima. When he can get them flown in and finishes a house he will test the lifting requirements. He can load cement sacks to substitute for people."

"Make sure he tests at least twice the expected weight load. Also, test your lift capability a thousand feet higher than the plateau. You might want to carry the cement in a second helicopter to the test site. Remember, don't go near the Preserve. Go north of Aconcagua."

"Don't worry, Roy," Mark was answering the phone and held his hand over the mouthpiece, "Chuck is much more conservative than you are. He will also test for the loss of lift if the weather turns bad and a low-pressure cell moves in. Bad weather translates to loss of one thousand feet in operating altitude." Mark returned to the call he was holding.

"That was Hector, the operations manager in Punta Alta. Maximillian has arrived and is changing into his new clothes. He should be here in a few hours."

"Good, I have to call General Parker to arrange for some smart bullets, tranquilizers and some support from the Argentine Air Force. We will get them to fly the captives off the plateau. As far as they will know, GOE is extricating some remote villagers from the path of an erupting volcano as a gesture of good will. I think you can get the Commandante to come up with the humanitarian insight and make the request for support from GOE. He will be a hero."

"No problem. When should we start torching the nets?"

"Why not tonight? Let's make a pass each night and watch to see how fast they put up new ones and if they leave the captives in the gardens without the net cover. Also, starting tomorrow can you put a seismic team on the plateau west of the Reserve and far enough away to avoid confrontation. Start a series of seismic tests. Give the area a good thump every hour on the hour until we are done. I want the seismic explosions to become part of the background noise of the Mapinguari world. We can also use the data to support the mapping of the tunnels. The WIGS staff has already been doing some mapping. They can always use more data."

Mark met Maximillian when the helicopter landed. He explained that an earthquake the night before had caused dirt to slide into site where the bones had been found. The supervisor and bulldozer operator were there clearing the fallen debris. It would be another hour before the bones could be reached.

Roy and Juan were above the pit reviewing maps of the canyon area. Mark and Maximillian walked down the bulldozer track leading to the lower pit. Mark yelled and waved. Juan waved back.

"Juan, where do you think the sharpshooters should be positioned?"

"Won't know until you get pictures with the nets burned out."

"Good answer. Let's go down and see Maximillian."

"Wow, right out of the pages of *EQ*," Roy said shaking Maximillian's hand.

"What's EQ"?

"Explorer's Quarterly. The magazine for the fashionable anthropologist. The source of what to wear in the field and at award ceremonies. I'm pulling your leg, Max. You look great."

"Mark says the bones were buried in a landslide."

"That blue ribbon is over the find. It will be a couple of minutes at most."

"Okay, come on over," Mike Swersey yelled.

Maximillian picked a small canvas bag filled with plastic bags, dental picks, brushes of different stiffness, a digital camera, magnifying glass, tape measures, cord which alternated in color every foot, folding wooden ruler and other tools of the trade and walked to Mike. The white cap of the skull was flush with the bank. Max stood there and nervously touched the bone.

Juan whispered to Roy, "I think he is going to have an accident in his pants."

Roy smacked him on the back of the head.

Maximillian Schnell unfolded the wooden ruler and stood it vertically to the left of the skullcap. "Roy, here is my camera. Would you get a picture of this?"

Roy photographed Max, the skullcap and the ruler.

Max climbed onto the terrace covering the find and marked off the areas where he thought they should dig. "Do we have anybody who can remove the dirt above the skeleton?"

Mike tossed a shovel to him. Max held the shovel and looked at Mike as if to say he was the director not a laborer.

Roy and Juan grabbed shovels from the bulldozer and climbed up to Max.

"You should break the ground as a ceremonial gesture. Mark will take your picture. Here, you will need these gloves."

"Oh thank you, Roy. You are right." Maximillian put on the gloves and pushed the shovel into the dirt. Mark snapped the picture. Maximillian started digging shovel after shovel.

"It is just a question of how to get people started," Roy said to Juan.

Maximillian dug for an hour before he staggered and sat down.

Roy took the shovel. "Relax Max, I think you were a little nervous about this whole thing. Mark, can you run a compressor hose down here? We can blow the overburden off without hitting anything with a shovel."

The outline of the skeleton slowly emerged. Roy had nozzle control that allowed him to concentrate the airflow to burn a hole or cut like a torch. He was able to cut away the rock all around the skeleton until it looked like a carving standing out from a wall at a museum.

"Just like Michelangelo, it is a matter of removing the rock from around the being inside," Roy said.

Before he started to cut the rock from under the skeleton Max indicated he wanted pictures. Maximillian knelt beside the ancient body with a large artist's brush in one hand and a dental pick in the other. Roy took pictures from several angles.

The individual had fallen face down with its right arm extended and the left hand in front of its mouth. Both legs were straight.

Mark wrote some numbers and the date on a slate and placed it next to the skull and took a picture.

"What is that for?" Maximillian asked.

"Global Positioning Satellite coordinate. Now you have a record of the exact location of your find within three centimeters."

"My find?"

"You are the anthropologist of record."

"But you found it."

"History will remember you for identifying it. All we did was find something unusual. You are the one who dated it and named it."

"I haven't done that."

"You will. Get back to work," Roy said, "So we can do what we have to do."

"Mark, do you have any fossil dating equipment?"

"We do in Punta Alta. Roy can insert a plank under MAX Jr. here and excavate the rest of the binding matrix. We can fly it and you to our lab."

"MAX Jr.?"

"It's easier to talk about things if they have names."

An hour later Max and MAX Jr. were on a helicopter to Punta Alta. Five hours later Mark got a call from a technician in Punta Alta.

"Max is drunker than a skunk and MAX Jr. is 10.5 million years old."

"Okay, we have to get Max and Max Jr. to Wallace Images and close this place down. As an antiquities site it can't be used to build a deep space tracking station so our project has ended. The owner of the property is going to close the area to foreigners until he understands what is in it for him. That will take a year and a half. Mike can have the hole filled in by tomorrow night. The sod will be replaced."

Roy called Eugene Langley and explained the proceedings of the past two days and the extraordinary finding that Maximillian had uncovered. Eugene was to orchestrate the publicity of the finds and indicate that the site was confidential for several reasons. That way when professional rights had been secured and landowner and government clearances were available, the site might be opened for further exploration. Roy also explained that one photo had GPS coordinates on it and that it should be erased.

The day after Maximillian returned to Seattle Mark indicated that a steel shed had been built and another was in progress. High altitude lifting tests had been made using enough sand bags to represent twenty one-hundred-pound people. The shed was stable at two thousand feet below the helicopter with the thrusters working automatically.

A team of twenty-one sharpshooters had been practicing shooting golf balls scattered on the floor of a remote canyon at 15,000 feet near Bogota for a week. The training was described as a joint effort in drug traffic control training. What was important was the shooters acclimatization to high altitude. Acclimatization increases the body's ability to absorb oxygen. In a stressful situation at high altitude it was going to be necessary for the marksmen to have steady aim and not be gasping when breathing.

For three days Roy and Juan watched the Mapinguari rebuild their nets that were burned the night before. Each day fewer nets were installed. On the third day only nets over the gardens in two canyons were replaced. Those nets appeared to come from tube openings high on the canyon walls. "Those must be defensive nets that they are going to use for cover," Roy commented. "Two more days should tell the story."

The next day no new nets were installed and the sentries marched the captives into the gardens.

"Mark," said Roy, "I think it is time for everybody to get together. Have Jason issue a volcano watch notice to the Argentine and Chilean Governments. Have the Commandante request GOE support through his channels. Move the sheds to the plateau and bring the shooters down from Bogota. Have General Parker deliver the smart bullets."

Juan and Roy were sitting at their favorite outdoor restaurant waiting for the dinner. Mark walked up the street, stood in front of them and flashed that morning's New York Times. The headlines for July 13th read "Prominent Northwest Anthropologist finds 10.5 Million Year Old Skeleton In South America" and the article indicated that the major anthropology institutions around the world were claiming it had to be a hoax. The age had been verified at several recognized research centers and is not disputed. The governments in Kenya, Ethiopia, Tanzania, and South Africa were asserting that the findings were stolen from Africa and taken to South America, then claimed to be found. Dr. Maximillian Schnell, Director of RENGCA, said he was not at liberty to disclose the site, raising suspicions of bone piracy. The article went on to note that, even if the site is a mystery, the credibility of many existing researchers has been challenged.

"A toast," Roy said standing and handing Mark a glass of wine, "to good old Maximillian."

In the morning light sharpshooters were deployed to locations that Roy, Juan and Mark had selected after studying photos for three days. They had studied the locations where Mapinguari had emerged from open tunnels and hidden tunnels. They had watched where the Mapinguari ran when an incendiary device surprised them. They watched where the hawks nested and flew when called.

The Argentine Air Force had four helicopters. They were stationed three miles south of the Preserve and could not see the rim of the canyons. GOE had two high altitude cargo helicopters and a gunship. There were two unmarked U.S. Air Force gunships. General Parker was in one of them. He had personally delivered the tranquilized smart bullets to Roy. All the helicopter blades were turning slowly.

GOE helicopters would extract gardeners from the canyon floor and transfer them to the Argentine helicopter site. The Argentine helicopters would then carry them to Punta Alta.

The net over the opening into the cave in the first canyon opened. Two sentries walked into the uncovered field and looked around. A third sentry herded six captives into the garden. Three sharpshooters pulled their triggers. There was no sound from the silenced rifles. The Mapinguari collapsed to the ground. A hawk dropped off a ledge one hundred feet above the cave entrance and started a graceful glide toward the opposite side of the canyon. There were no sounds as the bird suddenly plummeted straight to the ground and dropped in front of a gardener who immediately hit it with his stick.

As the hawk was falling, a large shiny object dropped from the sky at the west end of the canyon, corrected its fall and slid to the ground fifteen feet in front of the first gardener. The door in front flew open and two ominous looking black-clothed men emerged. They wore flack jackets, helmets, visors, heavy boots and armor covered pants. There was no speaking. One of the figures ran into the garden and shoved the emaciated gardeners toward the opening. In less than thirty seconds the silver house rose into the sky and disappeared.

At about the same time the same procedure was occurring in the next canyon three miles north. The sharpshooters immobilized the sentries. In this canyon there were three sentries in the garden and one at the opening to the lava tunnel. No hawks appeared. The steel box landed and the black-clothed warriors found they could move twelve gardeners into the box. One of the warriors noticed a skull on a stick at the end of the garden, and a book. He raced for them. The sharpshooter watching the entrance to the tunnel saw a Mapinguari with a raised spear rush out and pulled the trigger. The Mapinguari dropped as it released the spear. The spear struck the warrior in the leg, slicing through the kevlar armor as he picked up the book. He hopped back to the box. The other warrior stepped out, cut the long end of the spear off with a rapid swing of a machete and pushed his wounded partner into the box on top of the huddled gardeners. The box rose into the air to the west and south.

The box that had been emptied of its first round of passengers had returned and descended into the canyon to pick up the remaining gardeners without incident.

General Parker, hearing that a man was down, sent a replacement to meet the wounded man at the drop off zone. The wounded warrior was taken to the General's helicopter. Before accepting medical treatment, he insisted the skull and book be given to the General.

"Roy, we have found your missing Enrique Salivare and his diary."

"How is he?"

"He is auditioning for a part in Hamlet."

"Which?"

"Yorik."

"Understood. What about the diary?"

"Haven't had a chance really to look at it. It seems to start the day he returned to Punta Alta after being rescued and ends with a bloody page dated yesterday. I have no idea how they stripped his skull so clean so fast."

The shooters from the first two canyons were deployed to the third and fourth canyons. Roy was watching, scanning the canyon rims from the satellite through a remote link to WIGS. He had had WIGS preprogrammed for pattern recognition. As the first flying cabin approached the third canyon the warning light on his console blinked. The screen zoomed in on seven hooded figures approaching a group of shooters. "Fisherman!" he said into his microphone, "Top of Third canyon."

A helicopter with a large reel dropped down above the monks, releasing a net that skirted along the canyon surface under the feet of the monastic specters, then rose. The monks were bunched up in a tear-shaped ball. The helicopter returned to the first canyon, lowered the monks two thousand feet to the ground and released the net.

Extraction of captives from the third garden proceeded without injury to the warriors. Two gardeners were injured when spears pierced the tempered quarter-inch steel plate of the second cage.

Monks, or hawks or some other form of communication had prepared the Mapinguari in the fourth canyon. Almost immediately after the gardeners were pushed into the garden, sentries started to herd them back into the tunnel entrance. Every time a sentry ran into the garden it was tranquilized. Two shooters where killed by spears thrown a half a mile uphill. Mapinguari were in half a dozen tube openings throwing spears at the silver boxes. Gravity catapults had unerring accuracy. Two more shooters barely escaped injury when the rocks they were behind were split by a spear. Enough of the projectile's energy was absorbed to prevent penetration of their flack jackets. Four gardeners were killed when spears sliced through both sides of the cage. The two cages looked like porcupines with a dozen hand thrown spears in each.

When it became apparent that the cages were under attack they were rerouted. The occupants were placed in GOE helicopters and then flown to the Argentine helicopters. The crews from the BelGeo helicopters were taken to GOE helicopters for extraction. Mark thought he had a better chance at talking to them about what they had seen and reaching some form of agreement about their not talking about the Mapinguari to the press. Mark's primary interest was in determining if they had gained access to the two DNAS units that Mapinguari had when the BelGeo helicopters were captured. He concluded that BelGeo knew nothing about the DNAS.

The total operation took less than an hour. The only Mapinguari that might have been killed were those that fell three hundred to five hundred feet from the opening after being tranquilized.

That night at a GOE lodge a celebration party was held. "Well, General," Marked asked, "how do you want the war of the Mapinguari to be described?"

"I don't," he said. "You have to give them credit. They are an ingenious, resourceful and fierce people. Er, they are people, aren't they?"

"No, General. They are not."

After the party disbanded, Roy took Henry's skull and diary to his room.

March 29. Escaped a band of human like creatures. The creatures that Roy Graham and Mark Stark call Mapinguari chased them down a river. Roy and Mark had rescued several people that had been captured by the Mapinguari. I was with a support group that met them to escape on rafts. The Mapinguari killed one of the people who had been rescued. At the point where it looked like we would all die at the hands of the fierce band a helicopter arrived and shot them. I stole a head that was floating by. After a cursory look at the head I thought it was not human and resembled no creature I have ever seen. A helicopter took all the people that had been captured and now rescued. Several of them talked about their bizarre capturers and how they used gold and silver to catch helicopters. They apparently have a lot of gold.

April 5. Returned home. It was good to be home with Elmira again. If I can get a job with another company, then we can admit that we are married. Maximillian is gay and paranoid about nepotism.

April 6. Elmira has looked at the skull. She says it is not human. She knows more about anatomy than I do. She will do an autopsy.

April 9. Elmira has found the brain to be twenty percent smaller than Homo sapiens. The corpus callosum, the linkage between the two hemispheres was filled in, or larger, like Einstein's that made for a more efficient interaction between brain functions. The temporal lobe area associated with hearing larger and different. The portion of the frontal lobe some people think associated with ESP is percentage wise much larger than humans. The other parts of the frontal lobe associated with emotions and reasoning were smaller. There is magnetic tissue in the inner ear. They could probably navigate by the earth's magnetic field in the dark as well as by sound. An unusual sinus cavity looked like an echo chamber for emitting high frequency sounds. Its ears were not unusually large but did have features that might enhance sound at higher frequencies and the section of the parietal lobe linked to sensory signal processing was large. She indicated that the motor cortex was smaller and thinner than in humans. We need to do more study. The severing of the head destroyed the brain stem and some of the cerebellum. She thought the cerebellum involved in learning motor skills was larger. She was very excited about the skull.

She is going to get Laney Smith to do a DNA analysis with the understanding that he not divulge the source.

April 11. Laney Smith invited Elmira and me to dinner at Canles. He expressed a need to know more about the source of the DNA and he would do anything to help either of us. We told him about our marriage. He said he could arrange for me to get a good job with a company he was familiar with. He said he understood the problems working with Maximillian. He thought him an egocentric opportunist that grabs all the glory from GENXPLR if there was a find or discovery.

April 12. BelGeo, a Belgium exploration company representative, called me indicating they were looking for an anthropologist familiar with South America. He offered twice what I make at RENGCA. Elmira thought it might be a good idea. I called the BelGeo rep and accepted their offer. He wanted to know when I could leave for South America. I told him in a couple of days.

April 14. I tell Maximillian that I am leaving.

April 15. Met Roy Graham and Mark Stark in Laney's office. I didn't tell them I was going back to Punta Alta.

May 1. Leaving Punta Alta to go above Preserve. BelGeo is interested in the gold and silver I told them about. I indicated there were some fierce inhabitants in the canyon. They said they had enough fire power.

May 2. Our helicopter snagged a branch or something, looked like a net and we crashed landed in the bottom of the canyon. The pilot was killed. The creatures ate him in front of us. They cracked his skull open and they ate the contents like custard. All I can remember is vomiting and passing out.

May 5. I think today is the fifth. One of the BelGeo people said I had been unconscious for three days. I hit my head when we crashed. The stench in here is terrible. It makes me gag every time one of them passes by.

Another BelGeo helicopter has crashed. Two people killed in the crash. The creatures ate them in front of us.

They are barbaric but fascinating. Everybody is deprived of clothing and whipped and forced to work in the garden. For some reason they let me keep my journal and write. They seem to have a stockpile of pencils.

May 6. When I write one or two watch me. They are four feet to five feet tall, probably weigh 100 to 130 pounds, they are extremely sinewy and incredibly strong. They shy away when I try to show them how to write. I miss Elmira. I don't even know if she knows I am missing.

May 7. I did a sketch of a garden and the net overhead. One of them brought me a piece of the net. It is filled with gold and silver in both thread and pounded pieces.

May 8. I am not sure what I saw. Three of them sat around a flat round stone and seem to concentrate on a spot. The stone started to flake away like it was burning.

May 9. They move through the tunnels like bats. They send out high frequency calls. If I hang on to a tuft of hair on the back of one they guide me through a pitch black labyrinth.

May 12. I got lost somewhere in the dark. No food or water for a long time. I am freezing all the time. No clothes. I wish I could be more like them and get around. One of them found me. It was good to be back into the garden.

May 18. I think they realize I cannot see in the dark like they can. Today they took me to a connection between two of the caves we are in and lit a torch of pitch. They ignited it by focusing on it. The showed me how they have wheels that can be rolled between slots in the walls to block off the flow of water into a tunnel or to divert water into a tunnel. The tunnels appear to be lava tubes left over after a volcanic eruption.

I agonize over Elmira. She must know something is wrong. I hope she isn't too distraught.

May 19. They showed me more connections between tunnels and allowed me to sketch. One of them holds the pitch torch while I draw.

May 20. We walked forever. I thought my legs would fall off. We went to the top. We emerged on a high plateau. There were four monks there. I don't think they were entirely human. My guides and monks seemed to do a lot of talking. Clicks and squeals. Nothing I have heard before except whale recording and bat signals at slow speed. I looked at the monks and was beat to my knees.

They showed me the path of the water from the surface. All the water flow from the melting snow and rain is controlled through the tunnels to the rivers below. They can change which tubes will feed the waterfalls in the valley outside.

May 22. They are truly ingenious. They showed me a paddle wheel system to raise water several hundred feet through a network of catching basins that fed into a paddle wheel that raised water to the next basin.

May 24. They brought me the generators from several captured aircraft. I indicated on some drawings that if they turn the armatures they could generate electricity. They have no concept of electricity.

May 25. They found a piece of a turbine that they placed in water passing though a trough. I think they relieve themselves in the trough. The water made the turbine spin. They made an association with the spinning turbine and the generator drawing I had made. They made the generator work. I thought they would kill me when one of them got a shock.

May 26. They are having shocking parties. They take turns putting finger, feet, or their penis structure between the terminals.

May 27. They found out that humans don't like to get shocked and seem to enjoy the screams. Almost like children pulling the legs off of bugs. I haven't seen any children or female creatures.

May 28. They killed a gardener today with the generator. When they realized he was dead they ate him. They forced me to eat a scoop of brains from the poor soul. I have never been so repulsed or so exhilarated. I don't know what is happening to me. I don't know what Elmira would think of me now.

May 30. I found a light bulb in a pile of electronics and other items. One device is labeled DNAS and looks like a Buck Rogers space gun. When I picked it up my guide hit me so hard I couldn't stand up for a while. He let me take a light bulb and some wire.

June 2. I connected the light bulb to the generator. When the light went on they jumped back so fast I thought I had set off a bomb. They slowly crept back to the bulb. I showed them that when the wire was disconnected the light went out.

June 4. I wired about one hundred feet of a tube with bulbs lit by the generator. I drew a picture of Elmira's head by the light.

June 5. My guide saw my drawing of Elmira and motioned that he wanted me to complete the body. He was agitated when I started to draw clothing. I finally had to draw her as a nude. The creature went nuts, jumped around and ejaculated.

June 7. The lights were on in my little section of cave. Several of the creatures came in with my guide. They had with them what appeared to be females. They all coupled in very strange ways. I don't think they have ever coupled in the light.

June 8. My guide brought one of their females and forced me onto her. I find it hard to admit what happened. When I was allowed to withdraw he smelled her vaginal area and grunted and left. She stayed.

June 10. I am truly damned to hell. I can not escape this creature. She nearly castrates me until we couple

June 15. Sam, my guide, I find using a name more human. So much of that has been lost. Sam took me across the garden into a series of these lava tubes. We emerged in another canyon. There was another group of creatures and more gardeners. One of the gardeners was a woman. She was naked and smeared in feces. She looked like she was pregnant. These creatures in this canyon seemed like a different group or family.

June 18. Sam has taken me to yet another canyon and a different family. Tonight I drew a picture with five canyons and indicated where we are now and the two canyons we visited. I gestured that we would go to the fourth and fifth. He indicated we go to the fourth and he scratched out the fifth. It appears there are four canyons and four families.

June 20. Life seems to be one of survival: mending nets, tending the gardens, hunting. I haven't seen any grooming patterns with the others or with Gertrude. Except for the orgy like gathering, the one night with the lights on, I have seen nothing that might be called socializing. I haven't been able to discern any form of group, colony or hive hierarchy. How they organize tasks is a mystery. Of course, I really haven't figured out their language or even their means of communication.

June 24. Something has happened. After my coupling last night with Gertrude, the name I have given to the female creature, Sam sniffed her and yelled like a banshee. Another creature entered and smeared feces on her. I think it was some of mine. This seemed to be a way of marking. Gertrude left.

June 25. Gertrude has not returned.

June 26. No Gertrude. It was nice having her here if only for a little extra warmth. Her skin is leathery with some patches of hair. They are warm blooded, near 96 degrees. They also seem able to hibernate and slow down their pulse.

June 27. Sam indicated that the net with the gold and silver blocked the view from the sky of flying creatures. I guess he means helicopters. For fortification, these nets are used to block detection from the air. They also can close the openings to the canyon with thick stone slabs that are dropped into place in slots on the walls. There was no mechanism to raise these slabs so they were allowed to drop through the floor into the canyon to open the passage. A new blocking stone would be moved in from above the opening.

Openings in the canyon walls that were the source of dazzling waterfalls could also be used for battle stations. The water would be diverted upstream into spillway tunnels that lead directly to the river below the garden area. The spillways are used as an irrigation system for the garden. It was used to prevent flooding of the gardens during seasonal storms and spring thawing of the upper snowfield and to store water for dry periods.

June 29. Sam took me to a place that might best be called a foundry. We traveled a great distance and came to a place that was a geological contact between the lava and what appears to be granite. There were ten of them extracting mineral from the rock. Sam showed me veins of gold. They also had silver they were working with but I didn't see the source. There must be another area. They are able to fracture the rock around the gold vein by focusing on it. Some of the gold is so pure they are able to pound it into shape. Several of them focusing on ore are able to melt the gold and work it out.

They made me carry what felt like fifty pounds of gold when we returned. We came back through a cavern that opened to the canyon. There was enough light for me to see that this was where they made nets. About twenty Mapinguari were weaving flattened pieces of gold and silver and wire and thin metal from aircraft they had captured into a fabric of hide, and vines. They made holes in the metal with sharp flint-like tools and sometimes just focused and burned holes in the metals. I don't think all of the strips of hide came from animals.

July 5. I asked Sam where Gertrude was. He waved. I am not sure to what. I drew some pictures showing our location, scenes of coupling and another circle to indicate where the females go. He has started to draw. He drew another circle. There appear to be nursery caves. Females with successful coupling within their group go to one nursery. Coupling of them with a human female results in the woman eventually being moved to a different type of nursery. Coupling between human males and female creatures involves a third nursery.

I do not know what their gestation period is. The offspring are kept in nurseries until they are sixty pounds or so. I do not know what kind of training they receive.

July 7. Sam took me to the surface of the plateau again. The monks were there. I was allowed to see them disrobed. They are some freakish combination of human and creature. Apparently there is enough commonality in DNA to allow some cross-species survival. Some had features I have seen in the general population of Mexico City.

I don't know if the monks are from human females or creature females.

July 8. I have not found out what happens to the Mapinguari, if they are injured nor have I detected any diseases or malformations other than the monks. I might not be able to identify a diseased creature if I see one.

July 9. I have watched for some time the ability of Sam and others to communicate with animals especially falcons. Falcons are captured as chicks and raised. The shrilling sounds that Sam makes have imprinted on his falcon.

July 12. These creatures seem to have a large thoracic cavity and can generate very low frequency sounds. I have seen standing waves in pools of water when Sam appears to be grunting. The distance between the peaks of the waves varies from three to ten feet. After he makes his gesture he will seem to be listening and I see a different pattern of waves. Elephants, whales, Okapis and some rhinoceros are capable of generating low frequency vocalizations - below the range of human hearing - that carry long distances. Sam and the others seem to have this capability.

Having made the observation that the creatures might be using long wave communication, I understand why they get agitated before there is an earthquake.

They also have been agitated when thumping sounds come down from the surface. There have been periods since I have been here that there were thump-ing sounds like explosions on the surface every hour or so for five or six hours.

Something burned the nets. The creatures are very agitated and busy replacing the nets. They have long cannon-like devices with a pallet that rides on a rail. The pallet is pulled forward by a falling boulder. The spears that are placed on the pallet are ejected when the pal-let reaches the end of the rail. With this gravity catapult they are able to send spears and nets across the canyon.

July 15. There has been a thumping sound every hour on the hour all day long for the past two days. The nets have been burned the last two nights. Sam and the others seem very agitated. They seem to be using more low frequency communication than usual, like they are talking to creatures in the other canyons.

July 16. The thumping sound has not let up. Sam is angry. He has been pushing me like I am the cause of the sound. Tonight the nets were burned and he tore out my lights. I am afraid something is going to happen. I haven't thought about Elmira for a long time. I think I should say goodbye.

CHAPTER 16
RESCUE

The plateau was cleared of seismic testing equipment and Mark retrieved the two DNAS units, which had been disassembled. The power sources were missing and the Scintillator screens were broken. By the day after the extraction of the captives there was no evidence on the plateau of any activity except for two large rocks that had been split by spears.

Juan and Roy sat under a canopy of grapevines at a table covered with a flower-patterned oilcloth on the planked porch of the town's cantina. The porch was three steps up from a wide compact dirt road that widened at the edge of the village and served as the Town Square. A rusty-wire fenced field was on the north side of the cantina. It was sometimes used as a soccer field and sometimes as a helicopter landing pad. The road came from the north. It widened as it passed in front of the cantina and turned southeast when it passed. Across the square were a house, the town store, an administration building, and a school and small medical center.

A fourteen-year-old girl in a colorful peasant's dress had just set a pot of coffee, a basket of flour tortillas, refried beans, scrambled eggs, fried ham, slices of melon and orange juice on the table. Roy was scanning the canyons with his laptop connection to WIGS.

Juan read Henry's diary. "I had better eat before I read any more of this. I'll lose my appetite."

"Henry did have an adventure didn't he," Roy said. "If he had lived longer he probably would have gone native."

The sun had been up for an hour and most of the town was still inactive. Roy and Juan preferred to have breakfast before the temperature rose and town activity stirred up dust in the road. They usually had lunch and dinner inside.

"Here comes Thunder," Roy said, gesturing to an old horse plodding toward the cantina from the south end of the square.

Every morning Roy and Juan had seen the ancient animal make its rounds to each of the garbage cans in the square. Thunder, as Juan had named him, was a horsehide covering bones. Its head seemed unusually large because there was little muscle mass left in its skinny neck. It plodded slowly up the right hand side of the road toward the square. Each step was a deliberate act of exertion. The motion of every bone could be seen under the dirty skin. The hipbones looked like they would push through the hide. Its back was steeply bowed and all its ribs were outlined by dust and stood out nearly an inch and a half.

Thunder's neck and head hung low as he plodded past the cantina toward the garbage can at the north end of the porch. He stopped when he reached the can and bumped it with his nose, raised his head to the top of the lid, pulled his lips back and grasped the lid handle in his teeth. He raised his head and threw the lid to the right and paused. Lowering his head into the can he grabbed the black plastic garbage bag in his teeth, raised his head up and to the left and shook the bag until it broke open and its contents scattered on the ground in a five foot circle. Thunder methodically went from scrap to scrap biting open wrapped garbage and nibbling at cans and wrappers. Satisfied that nothing remained, he plodded across the square to the garbage can in front of the next building and began his extraction process.

Juan returned to Henry's diary while he ate his breakfast. Roy studied the canyons while he ate.

During the course of their breakfast, Thunder made his rounds to the garbage can in front of each building and then plodded down the road to the south out of sight.

"It is worth the price of admission," Roy said after Thunder disappeared."

"I couldn't do that," Juan said.

"Couldn't do what?"

"Screw one of those things. Ugh!"

"I don't think Henry wanted to."

After a few minutes Roy ask Juan, "Based on what you have read, do you think he could have killed Elmira?"

"No way, boss. He really loved her. He didn't know she was dead, did he?"

The young waitress returned with toasted flat bread, a bowl of citrus marmalade and two steaming bowls of coarse, oatmeal-looking cereal covered with thick cream. Roy scooped some cereal onto the bread and took a bite.

"Juan, this is really good. Eat some more before you read something that ruins your appetite."

"Has that ever happened?" Juan said.

"Now that you ask, No."

"I had better call MacFarland at Seattle Homicide and let him know we found Henry."

Roy evoked an icon of a telephone on his monitor and keyed MACFARLAND, SEATTLE, POLICE,

HOMICIDE into the search field. He pressed the Enter key and heard the phone ring.

"MacFarland, Seattle Homicide, how can I help you?"

"Mac, this is Roy Graham."

"Hi Roy, where are you?"

"Somewhere in South America."

"Were you part of that rescue of villagers in some mountain valleys? Volcano or something is threatening them."

"No, but I heard about it. Say, Mac, remember the lady you found in the Arboretum?"

"Yeah, she worked for a fellow out where you go sometimes, out by DayBreak Star. Man, his former boss sure made the news, big time; found a ten-million-year-old stiff. I thought my cases were old. Apparently somebody did not like him finding the old bones. A bunch of demonstrators are out in front of his place. Fundamental religious types putting down evolution and calling the bones fakes. We figure it is one of them that shot him."

"Shot Maximillian?"

"That is his name."

"How is he?"

"Superficial wound but still attempted homicide."

"You were looking for her roommate, Enrique Salivare."

"That's right. You thought he might have skipped to South America. You are there. Did you find him?"

"Yes Mac, he has been found. He is dead."

"Case closed?"

"I don't think so, Mac. It turns out they were married and very much in love. He didn't know she was dead when he left town."

"Do you have any ideas who did kill her?"

"My suspicions run to another person where she worked. Not in the company she worked for, however. Dr. Laney Smith is the person. He is Director of GENXPLR. I was going to suggest he might be a threat to Maximillian."

"So you think this Dr. Smith killed Elmira Cohen and tried to kill Dr. Schnell?"

"How come you always try to get me to do your job Mac?"

"Okay, I'll put him on my suspect list and follow up."

"Thanks, Mac, put a guard on Maximillian."

"Why are you always telling me how to do my job, Roy?"

"Mac, I'd love to spend more time talking but you're a busy man. Talk to you later."

"Finished," Juan said, putting Henry's diary on the table. He scooped cereal onto his toast. "Did I hear you say Maximillian was shot?"

"Superficial wound. He will be okay."

"I bet Smith did it. In Henry's diary it sounded like Laney Smith didn't like Max."

After breakfast Juan and Roy walked to the GOE office. Mark was placing transparent tinted plastic overlays on top of a map that included the Preserve.

"Just finished talking to Jason who reported John Wellington's latest update on the volcano. He says ninety-eight percent chance within four days."

"Will that kill off those things?" Juan asked.

"Not if we can do anything about it," Roy said. "I think we should try to get them out before the eruption."

"How can we do that?"

"Mark, how has seismic Tomography analysis progressed?

"Between the earthquakes and the extraction diversion we had enough echoes to map the canyon tubes and the New York subway system. We have a detailed map of every tunnel in all four canyon areas.

"Can we put everyone to sleep with gas and carry them out?"

"Maybe not everyone but a good number of them. We run down the tubes with three-wheel All Terrain Vehicles, ATVs. The tubes are large enough. With small utility trailers we can probably carry eight at a time. Three trailers, five trips is 120. Four canyons give us a potential 480. That's close to Henry's estimate of the population."

"If we can extract them Roy, where do we put them?"

"They have to be isolated and we can't spend too much time getting them there. Our options are either an island or a large mine."

"Or both," Juan said opening a map of the southern Chile and laying in on top of a map of the adjoining area in Argentina. "I don't think we can find any uninhabited islands within flying range. It is 800 miles down the Chilean coast to the Archipelago de Los Chronos. There are islands there, but that is too far away."

"Mark," Juan asked. "Do you have any offshore drilling platforms that could be used?"

"We have three that are not being used in the Gulf of San Matias. They could hold three hundred and maybe squeeze in another 50. Still short on capacity."

Roy looked at Juan to see if he was going to add another question. Juan tilted his head suggesting it was Roy's turn. "How about boats? Are there any mothballed or decommissioned battleships or carriers that could be towed? We don't need engine capacity."

"There is a navy base in Buenos Aires. I'll check that out in a few minutes. Also, we have a tin mine 400 miles south of the Reserve."

Mark put his finger on the map Juan had placed on the table. He tapped the canyon area twice and ran his finger along an imaginary eight-inch line south to a red circle.

"Here," he said. "It would not be affected by the volcanic activity except for falling ash if the wind blows south. There is only one entrance and several ventilation shafts. It has about twenty miles of tunnel. Plenty of room. It is not fully operational. We only have a skeleton crew there. They could be moved without any big loss. How long do we keep them? How do we feed them? Will they all get along together? There are four groups."

"Let's go with the tin mine." Roy said.

"If we bring out six to ten Maps per pass through the tunnel on an ATV and we will have to make fifteen to twenty passes through the tunnels. We should probably use four ATV's in each canyon. Every time two ATV's drop off their loads at the canyon floor there will be a helicopter load."

"Maps?" Juan asked.

"My jaws get tired saying Mapinguari all the time, Map."

"That's easy," Juan smiled. "So how many helicopters do we need?"

"Doesn't that get influenced by how long they will be out after we gas them?" Mark asked.

"There is some new stuff that can suspend consciousness for seventy-two hours," Roy answered. "That is three days."

"That's for humans," Mark interjected.

"Rabbits, mice, monkeys, birds and bats," Roy responded. "Anyway we will find out won't we?" Roy smiled, "I just love the empirical approach."

"So," Mark said, "we have time to get them through the tunnels, into the canyon, load them into a chopper and fly 400 miles. That is, what? A four-hour round trip. Let's assume we average fifteen Maps per helicopter trip, we will need thirty trips. Let's try for a two-day evacuation or forty-eight hours. Each chopper can make twelve trips. That means we need three helicopters and crews operating continuously. They will need to refuel."

"A hell of an effort," Roy said. "I am glad you have deep pockets."

"You are cutting a good-sized hole in them you know."

"Understood. Let's go with eight choppers, sixteen crews and, two choppers to supply a fuel dump on the plateau. We'll need six ATV's and utility trailers for collecting Maps in the tunnels. Lots of batteries and headlamps. First group into the tunnels marks the tunnels with fluorescent paints and use different colored flares for tunnel status. We will need fifty or so cargo nets to carry them."

"Cargo nets."

"We can't chance them being inside the chopper even if they are asleep. Besides it will be easier to load and unload them."

"This is going to be rough," Mark said. "The volcano is expected to go off in four days. It will take a day and a half to prepare the mine, pull in the extra choppers, and stockpile the plateau with gasoline."

"Start the gas stockpile at the same time we go in to locate the sleeping beauties."

"How long do we wait after we drop in the sleeping gas?"

"The gas is for the most part heavier than air. When first released it will flow down the main passages. After a time it will expand and rise. It will go down the main passages and rise into higher ones."

"How will we know when we can go in?"

"Let's wait six hours."

"Why six hours?"

"It's more than five. I really don't know how long we have to wait. The only thing we know for certain is there is not a lot of time available."

Juan looked at his watch, Roy and Mark. "When do we start?"

"I'll start in a couple of minutes to round up gear. That will take thirty hours. Three hours before that we drop the gas, wait three hours and start the extraction, which will take forty-eight hours. We should be done in seventy-eight hours. That means we have a ninety-eight percent chance of having eighteen hours to spare. With luck the weather will hold until we start."

"What did he say boss?"

"Mark said we have to hustle our butts or we will get wet. Actually, there might even be an advantage to a little bad weather. If it gets cloudy it might keep the monks off the top."

"What bad weather?"

"The weather forecast," Mark answered, "is for heavy rain and gale force winds in two days. There is a low-pressure cell coming that already has a record low barometric pressure. What a contrast that will be with this gorgeous day."

"I had better call General Parker and have him send some of the sleeping gas," Roy said standing up. "Let's get started."

For two days Mark and Juan sat on the phone arranging for equipment. Roy worked at the landing field, packing nets and supplies into helicopters. Each helicopter was painted with a unique large two-digit number for identification. Colors were used to identify the purpose of the helicopter. Red was for refueling, blue for carrying Mapinguari, white for support staff at the mine.

The sky on the morning of the rescue was dull red. The cloud level had dropped to within three hundred feet of the top of the canyons. The helicopters bringing in fuel cans had to relocate to a lower valley south of the Preserve. All pilots were notified.

The first four helicopters to arrive carried crews wearing gas masks. They flew to the pre-designated GPS location to a tunnel entrance identified from maps and seismic Tomography. The crew jumped out, located the entrance, ignited four gas canisters, threw them into the entrance, then covered it with a rubber coated nylon tarp. Rocks were placed around the edges of the tarp to keep it from blowing in the wind or in the helicopter propeller draft.

The crew flew to the next cave entrance and repeated the process.

By the time all the cave entrances had been covered the cloud level had dropped to two hundred fifty feet.

For the next four hours there was a constant drone of helicopters flying to the fuel storage area and helicopters delivering ATVs and small trailers.

Roy had planned to monitor the rescue effort from Punta Alta on his laptop with a WIGS satellite connection. The cloud cover was too dense and no images were possible. He decided, instead, to fly to the plateau and monitor activity from there.

He arrived and had the pilot land a short distance from the first entrance to be accessed. He could see four ATVs towing small trailers and moving in a line toward the tarp-covered entrance. The first ATV driver held a basket filled with flares and cans of spray paint between the handlebars. At the entrance Roy was watching as the driver stopped and walked to the tarp. With binoculars Roy noticed that the tarp was bulging up in the middle, had pulled away from the rocks on one corner and was flapping up and down. He noticed that the driver did not have his gas mask in place as he lifted the tarp. Before Roy could press the switch on his radio, the driver pulled back the tarp and collapsed.

Roy yelled into the radio "Secure your gas masks."

Two other drivers ran to the aid of the fallen driver. They did not have their radios on and did not hear Roy's warning. They collapsed before they reached the first driver.

Roy called Mark and asked that the seismic detection systems be activated.

"Roy, I can turn them on but we don't have any thumpers, explosive charges, up there."

"Don't worry, we will thump. I need to know if the Maps have blocked off entrances to tunnels and what the source of the updraft is."

"What updraft, Roy?"

"The one blowing the gas back out of the tunnels."

"Roy, remember our trip to Jewell Cave near Mt. Rushmore, South Dakota?"

"Damn. You're right. Barometric winds." A number of years earlier, Roy and Mark had climbed Devils Tower in Wyoming. They had made a side trip to the Mt. Rushmore area and visited the Jewell Cave National Monument. Jewell Cave was believed to be one of the largest in the world in terms of total volume, even though none of the rooms was very large like those at Mammoth Cave in Kentucky. Roy had met a climber turned spelunker who had explored the cave system for twenty years. He estimated the volume of the cave by blocking the only known entrance with a door that had a circular opening that held a wind gauge and an air pressure gauge on the inside and an air pressure gauge on the outside. When the weather was nice and the barometer readings high, the air pressure deep in the cave, in the large rooms, in the tunnels and all the cracks in the rock slowly adjusted to the high pressure. When the weather turned bad and the air pressure outside the cave dropped, the high pressure inside the cave system eventually dropped as air escaped as wind currents through the cave entrance. Knowing the size of the hole in the door, measuring the velocity of the air moving through the hole, and the pressure difference between the inside and the outside of the cave he could measure how much air had moved out of the cave through the hole in the door. With that data he could estimate the volume of the cave.

Mark said, "I bet the same thing is happening here. The high pressure in the cave from the nice weather we have been having is forcing air out of the openings."

Roy told the pilot to raise the chopper three feet and let it drop to the ground, or better, to reverse the lift and force the chopper to the ground. The force of the helicopter hitting the ground was sufficient to generate a compression wave that traveled through the rock just as small explosions would.

After three thumps Roy asked Mark, "Did anything register on the Tomographer?"

"Yes."

Ray told the pilot to have all the helicopters do the same thing for ten minutes.

"Roy, you guys are creating a hell of a racket. We have been able to identify blockage at all the major tunnel exits and a number of blockages between the third and fourth levels of tunnels. The Maps blocked off the gas flow."

"Besides their blocking the entrances to their living chambers, we have barometric winds blowing the gas out of the holes we put it in. The weather has been nice for a week, and now the caves are decompressing."

"I hate to admit it, Mark, but we have been beat by a bunch of stone-age savages. General Parker will never let me live this down."

"So what do we do?"

"Leave everything and get out of here. Sound the bugle, wave the goddam white flag and all that stuff."

"Fuel dump, ATV's?"

"Leave them."

Three hours later all the helicopters were on the GOE airstrip.

Roy, Juan and several pilots where sitting in a hanger drinking coffee at a makeshift table when Mark came out of his office.

"Jason just called from Seattle. He says pull out," Mark said. "Wellington heard the volcano throat burp. It will probably erupt in another half-hour or so. We couldn't have saved anybody if we'd stayed up there. In fact if we had stayed we would have been killed."

"I wonder if we see any high altitude disturbances?" Roy said as he went to get his laptop and connect to WIGS. He returned and booted into WIGS. The satellite could see only clouds.

One of the pilots noted that the storm was massive. "What is the cloud level?" He asked. "My guess is 30,000 feet. Even the disturbance of wind going over Aconcagua at 23,000 feet doesn't register. Oh my word, look at that."

There were several gasps as a massive black cloud mushroomed and boiled up from the dense flat plain of clouds. A line of numbers appeared on the monitor to the right of the expanding cloud. 30,000, 35,000, 40,000, 45,000.

The ground shook and tools fell of the walls, two small planes fell off jacks, a fuel line ruptured and flames broke out in one corner of the hanger.

An enormous explosion shook the building and echoed off the clouds. It took a second or two for most people to realize the explosion was from the erupting volcano five hundred miles away. Several fire extinguishers were deployed and the flames squelched. The altitude of the cloud had reached 75,000 feet and was drifting east toward Punta Alta, riding a jet stream over the top of easterly-moving storm clouds. Five minutes later the rain turned to black mud and there was not a hint of daylight. Automatic light sensing switches turned on the emergency lights. The lights flickered and went out. It was pitch black for a few seconds before a standby generator started.

Two small corrugated metal covered shacks collapsed under the weight of accumulating muddy volcanic ash. During flashes of lightning, birds could be seen, lying on their sides, trying to lift their wings in the three inches of black mud covering the runway.

"Turn off all internal combustion engines." Roy warned. "If the silica in the ash is sucked into the combustion chambers it will eat the cylinder walls."

Before the generators were turned off one pilot noticed his helicopter was still running, the blades turning slowly. He had planned to leave after a cup of coffee. He ran toward the helicopter and slipped and fell on his face, his right arm stretched forward. He didn't move and by the time Roy, Juan and two others walked carefully to him he was completely covered with ash. Another pilot turned off the helicopter engine.

Juan looked at Roy as they picked up the fallen pilot. "Have you seen this before?"

"Yeah, ten million years ago."

The generators were turned off. The only light anybody had to find their flashlights with was the constant flashing of lightning.

Mark said, "We had better get out of this hanger, I don't think the room will take the load of ash."

Everybody moved to a stone walled building with a steeply pitched roof. The hanger collapsed when the wet ash was nine inches deep. Over twelve inches of ash fell while the ash cloud passed.

Roy asked WIGS to contact Jason on videophone. Roy explained he still had two hours of battery left in his laptop and would have to use it sparingly.

Jason provided some information on the intensity of the earthquake, how far away it was felt, the estimated volume of ash and the expected depth of the lava flow that would descend on the upper levels of the Preserve. "Since you didn't get any of them out, are they gone now?"

"You know, I've been wondering about that," Roy said. "They showed us that they are survivors. If you think about it, they are living in caves that are lava tubes through twelve distinct lava beds. I bet they have been through these lava flows a number of times."

"How do they survive this?" Jason asked.

Everyone was listening to Roy.

"This is speculation. Let's say they close off the tunnels below five hundred feet. The top five hundred feet of overburden acts like an insulator so they stay cool for fifteen hundred feet of caves. They have food and water stored. They can stay in there for years."

"I would also imagine," Roy continued, "that the top five hundred feet heat up, expanding the air in the tunnels and cracks in the walls. The expanding gas tries to escape the openings on the surface, which is being covered with flowing lava. The expanding gas pushes into the lava, which is already cooling as a big gas bubble. The flowing lava stretches the bubble, which eventually becomes another tunnel. As the lava cools the advance stops, and the area above the hole where the gas escaped is pushed open."

Mark says, "Are you suggesting that the lava flow from the eruption of the volcano adds another level to the Map hotel?"

"That is what I am suggesting, Jason." Roy said, "There should be enough after-shocks to give you some seismic data."

"Right."

"Jason, let us know when things clear up down here if the Preserve has a new layer and a new set of tunnels."

"Will do."

"Ain't empiricism grand," Roy said and raised his cup of coffee as a salute.

CHAPTER 17
LANEY

"Mac"

"Hi Roy. You still in South America?"

"No, I am in the Firehouse. We got in early this morning. I dropped Juan off at his place. It sure looked like his wife was ready for him. I don't think any of the neighbors saw her outfit or lack of it and called the police."

"I thought he got divorced."

"That was from his third wife. Mac, I called to find out what has happened with the Elmira Cohen case and Maximillian's shooting."

"We went out to the complex on Magnolia Bluff and talked to Dr. Laney Smith. We didn't charge him with anything or even suggest he was a suspect. We asked the usual questions about where he was before the body was found, who he thought might have a reason to kill her and so forth. We also talked to other members of the staff. He got agitated when we asked him not to leave town. I had to tell him twice he was not under arrest."

"He even tracked me down as I was coming out of Conrad Blankenstaff's office and was shouting he didn't kill Elmira Cohen. I had to explain to this Conrad guy that nobody was being charged yet."

"What would happen if you took him in for questioning? Take him downtown and find out the last time he saw Elmira. Also, find out if Henry was with her. Find out what restaurant they went to."

"You already know, don't you?"

"Yes but I want it to be official when you find out. Also, find out from him who or what BelGeo is."

"Okay, we will send a car for him now."

"I am going out to Wallace Images in a few minutes. I am curious to see if anything happens after he is picked up."

"Maximillian, how is the world's most famous anthropologist?" Roy entered Maximillian's office and gestured for Max to stay seated.

"Abused, confused and amused."

"How so?"

"Somebody shot me. They just nicked my arm-pit. Another inch or two and we wouldn't be talking. Somebody had the audacity to suggest it might have been Laney. God knows we fight a lot about budgets and he is jealous beyond belief about my success, but the two of us have kidded each other about these things for years. Deep down he is my dearest friend. I think a lot of people misinterpret our professional squabbling as personal issues."

"Besides, he told me to enjoy my famous fifteen min-utes because he had something that might be better than my 10.5 million year old boy. If he wants to upstage me, why would he shoot me?"

"Maybe to throw you off guard and have you as his witness."

"Don't be ridiculous, Roy. You read too many detec-tive stories."

"Roy, you and Mark gave me that find. Why?"

"We might have influenced events a little and might again, who knows, but you are the one who identified the find. There are other agendas. For one, the way we found the skeleton involves technology that Mark's company developed and is now classified by the mili-tary, so Mark doesn't want his company involved in the publicity. I personally do not want to get wrapped up with the hype. This is your field, you know the cast of international players, and you will have fun taking on the Creationists and every institution with a mummy or an old bone on display or in a closet."

"For the moment Max, we want to keep you alive and find out who shot you and most likely who killed Elmira."

"You think they are connected? I thought Henry killed Elmira."

"Yes. I think they were connected. Until a couple of days ago I also thought Henry did it. Now I have my doubts. We found Henry's body, or part of it, and his diary."

"Where?"

"I'll tell you later. I am going down and scratch a table."

"The Shrimp Scampi is great."

"Hold it a second, Roy, let me catch this call."

Maximillian answered the phone, sagged in his chair and hung up. "They just took Laney to the police station. Roy, he couldn't have done it."

Roy went to the cafeteria, said hello to a few people, and picked up a plate of the Scampi, a garlic roll, some greens and coffee and located a panel window overlooking Puget Sound. The panel was a display but it was the same view as the one that would be seen through a real window. A ferryboat was exiting Elliot Bay on its way to Bremerton. A jumbo jet was making its landing approach for Sea-Tac airport sixteen miles to the south.

"Mind if I sit with you?"

Conrad looked up at Roy, "Yes, sit. Good to see you." Roy reached across the table and shook hands with Conrad. "You have been a tremendous help the last few weeks. Don't know what we would have done without you."

"That is nice to hear. Thank you. I don't get a lot of that."

"What?"

"Recognition."

"How can that be. I will certainly let Laney know what a tremendous asset you have been. There are a couple things that can't be said but there should be a way of conveying appreciation for your contributions. Maximillian's find would not have been possible without your original identification of the pre-hominid DNA link. I think that within two years we can release that information. You will be famous."

Conrad flushed. He unbuttoned his collar and loosened his tie. "You think so?"

"Damn right."

"They arrested Laney."

"What do you mean? I just got here and hadn't heard."

"The police took him to the police station. I think they know he killed Elmira and shot Maximillian."

"You know, Conrad, I find that hard to believe. Why would he do those things?"

"I don't know. Maybe she had something on him that he didn't want her to tell anyone. He is really incompetent, can't do anything serious and then takes credit for the work of others."

"She doesn't work for him. What could she do for him?"

Conrad leaned forward and tried to talk low. He was trying to speak so nobody but Roy could hear and started wheezing. He sat up and took a deep breath, looked around to see if anyone was watching.

"Do you remember that tissue scraping that you and Mark first brought me?"

"Yes."

"Laney brought me a sample of the same stuff a week before you did. She had given him a sample the day before to test. She said she had badgered Enrique so much that he showed her something that would stop her haranguing. She asked Laney to analyze it for her. He doesn't know what we are doing here so he came to me. I ran the analysis for him. He knew she had something important. I guess she wouldn't tell him where the sample came from so he killed her with the statue."

"So you are suggesting, that, if he knew there was DNA from something really old that might have led to the rise of modern hominids, he might get his fifteen minutes of fame, as Maximillian calls it. Max did imply that Laney felt confident that he could eclipse Max."

"Right. Roy, if Laney doesn't come back. If he did it, who heads up GENXPLR?"

"The GENXPLR Board I imagine, James Wallace and six others who are really puppets to James. That's between you and me. I know that if I were James I'd pick you. You know the structure of GENXPLR and the technology and you have insight into what is possible."

"You know if they pick you as Director that you will have to get a physical."

"What?"

"Come on Conrad I've bugged you to get a physical for a year and a half now. Directors have to be healthy. You can't start wheezing at a Board Meeting.

"One last thing puzzles me, Conrad. I thought Henry killed Elmira. That was the rumor before I went to India. She died and he disappeared."

"It looked that way but Henry left town to go work for BelGeo. I saw Elmira in Laney's Porsche the night she died. I was coming in to work on WIGS. I'd have to check the WIGS schedule to get the time."

"BelGeo, who are they?"

"Laney had mentioned them once but I don't remember in what context."

"Conrad, I have to go. Be sure you get your physical. Goodbye.

"Thanks, Roy."

"MacFarland, Homicide."

"Mac."

"What's up, Roy?

"Can you bring Dr. Laney Smith back?"

"Can I? God I hope so. He is a piece of work and he is connected. An Aide to the Governor, two Senator's Offices and the Mayor have been rattling my cage. Can I? You tell me."

"I keep telling you, Mac, I am not going to do your job for you. I might make a suggestion now and then but that is all."

"What are you suggesting?"

"Take Dr. Smith back to his Office to collect any personal items he thinks he might need if he is going to spend a night or two in jail.

"Do I tell Dr. Smith that he is or is not under arrest?"

"Just tell him to get what he needs. If he thinks he is under arrest, leave it that way."

Roy walked to Eugene Langley's office. "Eugene Langley, I am glad you are free for a few minutes," Roy said without checking.

"Come in Roy. I want to hear all about your trip but things are a bit hectic at the moment. What is on your mind?"

"In a short while the police are going to bring Laney to his office. The story is, to get any items he might need for a stay at the police station. I want you to be there and to call in Conrad Blankenstaff. Raise the question of who is in charge while Laney is gone."

"Then what?

"Play it by ear."

"What are you going to be doing?"

"Listening. Gene, put your Dick Tracy watch on vibrate. I might want you to ask some questions. They will display on your watch screen."

"You have been reading too many detective stories."

"I have heard that."

The protestors dropped their signs and turned their faces away from the road as several police cars drove up to the Wallace Images gates. The officers looked uncertain when they first parked and walked toward the blank gray walled obelisk. They stiffened slightly when the walkway appeared in front of them and then the door appeared. "Yellow Brick Road," one of them muttered.

Lieutenant MacFarland and a sergeant escorted Dr. Smith to his desk. Four other officers stood in the hall outside the office. Eugene Langley entered the room and looked at Dr. Smith.

"Gene, please tell these gentlemen that I could not do what I am accused of."

"Laney, this thing is out of my hands. I am going to do everything I can. In the meantime I need to know who is in charge in your absence. Is Conrad okay?"

"I don't know why not."

Eugene pressed the intercom to Conrad's office and asked Conrad to come to Laney's office.

Conrad walked into the room looking over his shoulder at the officers in the hallway.

Eugene felt his watch vibrate and read the message.

"Conrad, you are in charge."

Laney had a confused look on his face that bordered on panic.

Conrad smiled. "It is about time. I knew you were incompetent and now the others will find out. When I show them what can be done here, this organization will get some of the credit it deserves. Now maybe I will get recognition for the work I have done for you."

Eugene looked confused. "What are you saying, Conrad?"

"Every time somebody asks Laney to do an analysis he brings it to me. He doesn't know how to do it. I do it and he takes credit."

Roy was listening to Conrad's heart which registered on the security system. His pulse rate was increasing. The faulty valve added a delayed blip on the screen. Roy typed *Like Elmira's sample* on the keyboard and pressed Function Key 3, which had been programmed to send output to Eugene's watch.

"Like Elmira's sample." Eugene said as a statement, not a question.

"That is a good example. If he had to do the analysis on his own he would never have known how important the sample was. I bet he hit her with her fertility statue when she wouldn't tell him where the sample came from."

Roy watched the proceedings in the room from the WIGS retina scanner in Laney's office. The scanner was really a general-purpose digital video input device. Retina calibration and tracking were only two of many possible uses. Monitoring activity in a room was another. He saw Lieutenant MacFarland's attention shift to full alert when Conrad mentioned the statue.

Roy signaled Eugene who responded, "Who got Henry his job with BelGeo?" Eugene asked.

"I did, who else? He said he wanted to leave Maximillian because Max was too cheap. I bet Laney is even cheaper. I called BelGeo. They offered Henry twice what he made here."

"Would she go out with you then?" Eugene looked toward the Retinal scanner and gave Roy a look that registered *Are you crazy.*

"She was ready to. I told her I knew about the sample; that I had made the analysis, not Laney. I told her I had BelGeo offer Henry a job and since he was no longer there maybe she needed a new roommate."

"Did you go to her apartment?" Eugene asked. He had picked up on what was happening.

"That's where I was when I told her I had gotten rid of Henry and she could have me. I am the best at DNA analysis and could help her with her career."

Mac was nodding his head. "Is that when you hit her?"

"Damn right. That bitch didn't know a good thing when it was offered. She called me a bald cretin."

"You idiot." Laney said. "They were married, she was pregnant."

"That can't be. She wanted me but just didn't know it. She would have learned."

"You are under arrest, Conrad Blankenstaff, for the murder of Elmira Cohen," Mac said. "Officer, read him his rights."

"You cannot arrest me. You need me." Conrad shouted. He was flushed and sweating. Roy watched Conrad's pulse rise to 150 and heard a ripping sound in a valve.

Conrad was gripping his left arm. He wheezed then gasped, "I know too much. I know Pandora's Box. I know about the ear. I know about the Maps, DNAS." Conrad died.

CHAPTER 18
ISSUES

Roy could tell from the caller ID on the phone that Mark was calling from Antarctica. "Mark, what are you up to?"

"They're back."

"Maps?" Roy asked.

"Only in the first canyon," Mark answered. "Since you gave us access to WIGS we have monitored the canyon every fifteen minutes for any change in patterns. The process is automated. It has been three weeks. This morning the pattern-change alarm sounded. WIGS happened to catch the initiation of a net launch. A line had already been strung across the canyon and a net was being drawn across. It took them two hours to get it set up."

"Wow. Any sign of prisoners?

"No. What are you going to do, Roy? Burn the net?"

"I don't know, Mark. There are a lot of issues. What do you think?"

"My boss wants me to get back to finding oil. You figure it out."

"Understood. Go find oil. I'll talk to you later."

The fire bell sounded twice as Juan rang the bell and entered the old fire station. "Come on up, Juan."

Roy had a number of aerial photographs and maps of the canyon area and the Preserve spread out on his drafting table. Juan looked at them for a while and asked, "We aren't going back, are we?"

"No, Juan. Relax. I am wondering how much area should be set aside for the Mapinguari. The informal Preserve boundaries aren't sufficient to protect them or developers that might work in that direction."

"You want them protected?"

"Not so much protected as left alone. The boundaries of the Preserve can be better defined and monitored to keep people out. You know that rumors of gold will drive a number of people crazy. I guess they have the right to become gardeners if they want to. In the long run it would be easier to catch intruders before they become Mapinguari property than to have to rescue them."

"How about the Mapinguari?" Juan asked.

"I am reasonably sure that they will not venture far from the canyons. The monks have never been known to be hostile. They are more like information gatherers."

"Can the monks be assimilated and act as interpreters?"

"Possibly, but to what end? Interpreters imply communication and that suggests change. Change doesn't mean leaving them alone."

"How will you know how they are doing?" Juan asked.

"How is your first wife doing?"

"I don't know, she is not my problem and as long as she stays away from me I don't care how she is doing. Why do you ask that?"

"If, Juan, the Mapinguari are not our problem, why should we care how they are doing?"

"Won't you get curious as to what they can do?"

"Absolutely, but that doesn't give me the right to interfere with their lives."

"How about all the mining companies, land grabbers and academics that like to stick their noses into everybody's business? How about the missionaries that will want to convert them?" Juan asked.

"Keep them out."

"How?" Juan asked. "Are you going to put a fence around the Preserve?"

"That might not be that difficult. The fence won't have wires. It will be electronic detection and satellite scanning. The major issue is getting the boundaries of Preserve recognized internationally. The upper reaches of the Preserve are open and easily monitored. Accessibility from below is very difficult. A variety of sensors can be deployed. Since anybody entering the Preserve will probably be armed they can be detected unless they are carrying plastic bullets and guns. They can be detected even with periodic scans since it will take them days by foot. It won't be like crossing the border at Tijuana. Aircraft can be detected. Missionaries have been eaten before and it will probably happen again."

"You're a dreamer Roy. Greed, curiosity and religious zeal are powerful forces."

"Juan, you are absolutely right. The best we can do is help clarify the boundaries and possible consequences and hope that nobody gets in there by accident."

www.ingramcontent.com/pod-product-compliance
Lightning Source LLC
Chambersburg PA
CBHW071311170626
46809CB00001B/406